CASCADE

ALSO BY CRAIG DAVIDSON

FICTION

The Saturday Night Ghost Club

Cataract City

Sarah Court

The Fighter

Rust and Bone

NONFICTION

Precious Cargo

CASCADE
STORIES
CRAIG
DAVIDSON

W. W. NORTON & COMPANY

Independent Publishers Since 1923

Copyright © 2020 by Craig Davidson
First American Edition 2021

For information about permission to reproduce selections from this book, write to Permissions, W. W. Norton & Company, Inc., 500 Fifth Avenue, New York, NY 10110

For information about special discounts for bulk purchases, please contact W. W. Norton Special Sales at specialsales@wwnorton.com or 800-233-4830

Manufacturing by LSC Communications, Harrisonburg
Production manager: Beth Steidle

Library of Congress Cataloging-in-Publication Data

Names: Davidson, Craig, 1976– author.
Title: Cascade : stories / Craig Davidson.
Description: First American edition. | New York, N.Y. :
W. W. Norton & Company, 2021.
Identifiers: LCCN 2021016247 | ISBN 9780393866902 (paperback) |
ISBN 9780393866919 (epub)
Subjects: LCGFT: Short stories.
Classification: LCC PR9199.4.D383 C37 2021 | DDC 813/.6—dc23
LC record available at https://lccn.loc.gov/2021016247

W. W. Norton & Company, Inc., 500 Fifth Avenue, New York, N.Y. 10110
www.wwnorton.com

W. W. Norton & Company Ltd., 15 Carlisle Street, London W1D 3BS

1 2 3 4 5 6 7 8 9 0

For Charlotte

CONTENTS

THE GHOST LIGHTS

Stars. Fractured star-sprays and burning constellations ... galaxies radiating like spokes on a wheel, their epicentres—the suns—dancing pinpricks of kaleidoscopic brightness.

Then: Black.

The steady trickle of salt water dripping in a sea-cave. Lurking behind it: the hiss of a serpent sidewinding over wet rocks.

"Uh ... *hwwwuuugnnh* ..."

... you were born into dread, my son ...

A fairytale giant has collected my blood in a glass globe he wears strung round his neck. The giant laughs, his paving-stone teeth flashing, as I beg for my blood back ...

A sudden, buzzing pinworm of pain corkscrews through me. The wire cools. It is someone else's pain now. I'm only holding onto it. Far off, the giant is still laughing.

Blink.

Snap to with a snort.

I'm suspended upside down, belted into the passenger seat of our car. A Volvo: boxy, brooding, Swedish. Snow is piled against the windshield; cold granules of sunlight petal through the shattered glass. Gravity pulls my knee-caps down; my feet are wedged beneath the glovebox and my wrists bent back against the roof upholstery.

"Dan . . ."

The airframe sparkles with powder from the deployed airbags. The Volvo has an embarrassment of them—a number that struck me as farcical in the austere showroom. Now the interior is draped with deflated alien spore-bags, satiny-white, and my lips are caked with xenomorph eggs. There's an acid burn in my sinuses—did I throw up? No: that's antifreeze. I've been at enough accident scenes to recognize the smell. It must be trickling through the vents with its greasy, burnt-animal stink.

I try turning my head—a wire buzzes with such inten-sity that it shocks a strangled scream out of me. In the rearview I catch sight of something inverted in the back-seat like a little hangman. A pocket-sized executioner with a white hood over his face. A cold lunar silence weeps from the driver's side. I can think of no good reason to look directly at that ghastly quiet next to me—*Why, when it would be so easy?* a sharp-toothed voice urges. *Just turn your head a smidge and . . .*

When I move my left arm, the pain is mammoth. I reach cross-body with my right hand to unlock the seatbelt. My fingers are senseless pegs riveted to my palm. I thumb the button but nothing happens. The lock's jammed.

The hangman in the backseat emits a consumptive snuffling like a Pekinese with a sinus problem. He broods back there—in every un-noosed neck he sees an opportunity lost.

The belt is cinched tight across my shoulder. My entire body feels like it's resting on one fragile joint. There's a Leatherman in the glovebox. I try to heel off my boot before realizing it's already gone: both boots must've been flung off in the ... my knee brushes the stereo knob and the cab fills with the insane screech of the Doodlebops, their helium voices turning cat-yowly before cutting out.

With one big toe, I pop the latch. The glovebox jars open, spilling oil-change receipts and the Leatherman, which strikes my incisors and floods my mouth with the taste of rolled nickels. I retrieve it from the roof and fumble the blade open. Blood pools in my skull; the pressure must be turning my face as red as skinned meat.

It's taxing work cutting through the belt. The wire buzzes hotly until the severed strap hisses through the belt's eyelet. I complete a graceless backwards somersault and in that frictionless second, my head swivels to force a confrontation with the scene I've been avoiding.

Ahhhh, breathes the sharp-toothed one. *Isn't that a treat.*

A tree limb is spiked through the Volvo's windshield; the safety glass is crumbled around the hole it made entering our world. The branch pierced the driver's-side airbag—shreds of white ballistic nylon still cling to its bark—before carrying on into Dan's . . .

Oh, I remember this tree. I'd seen it lurking within a copse of its brethren just off the unplowed corduroy road. A tree waiting on this very chance with one of its branches projecting at a perfect ninety-degree angle: a straight jab of oak encased in transparent ice, its end whittled by sun and wind until only the hardest stuff remained. The heartwood, it's called.

That branch is now married to Dan's face. His head is tilted back, his throat shorn by the wood running on its unbending plane: his neck and the branch form an inverted capital "T."

Later, maybe I'll have an opportunity to lie about how coldly I accept my husband's death. At the funeral home with Dan's pale-eyed father, both of us standing over his son's coffin. *I doubt I'll ever come to grips with it, you know?* But before the back of my skull even hits the dome-light I am reconciled to the fact, and moving past it.

I land on the stem of my neck, and my left side explodes in white-hot fireworks. I plant my feet on the windshield and push, snapping off the rearview mirror as I worm between the front seats to the little hangman suspended upside-down in his car seat.

"It's okay, baby. Mommy's here."

Charlie is fastened by a meshwork of straps with his head socked between two fabric bananas. When we drove home from the hospital with him two months ago, Charlie's head hung at a terrifying cockeyed angle on his neck. *Yikes, that looks painful,* Dan said. That afternoon he fixed the bananas in place.

My son's bib has flipped down over his face but when I lift it, his face is unbloodied and his eyes bright. He sits jack-knifed at the hips—he has the shocking elasticity exclusive to babies and Balkan contortionists—his bootied feet folding down to touch his forehead. He's so quiet it's easy to believe he's dead, but infants make you believe they're either dead or just about to die several times a day. The moment I reach for him blood begins to foam out of his nose, as if my fingertips released it. It bubbles up from the cups of his nostrils and falls the wrong way down his face to collect in his eyes. But my son doesn't make a sound.

Bracing one hand on his seat's carry-bar, I stretch my foot up to pop the release catch. The seat falls painfully onto my chest. Wheezing, I thumb one of Charlie's eyelids open: pupil dilated, the whites wormed with broken corpuscles. I probe his fingers through his tiny mittens, then move up each of his arms. Toes, feet, legs. Okay, okay, okay . . . I loosen the straps so he can breathe freely.

As a paramedic with the Niagara General Hospital, I've attended accidents like this. The first thing you learn is that you can't save everyone. You must cradle a brutal stone of expediency in your heart.

I rest with Charlie on my chest. Now that his nose has stopped bleeding, he roots at my breast through my jacket. Snow is piled at the Volvo's windows. Above the snow lies a slit of paling winter sky. The dashboard is lit, which means the battery's not dead. Okay. I thumb the window button; the glass rises into its rubber flap with Swedish precision. I inhale pulverizing, cold air. It's early December and the world is locked in an arctic freeze.

Digging with my elbows, I shove myself though the window. The snow is the dry powdery kind that falls during a cold snap. Unzipping my jacket, I slip a hand under my shirt. The wing-shaped bone running from my neck to outer shoulder is broken. The break-ends shift against one another to create a nausea-inducing buzz.

It's bearable. Now get moving.

This voice belongs to an ancient village hag who sleeps on the bones of her enemies.

I can chart the Volvo's path across the snow in the ashy late-afternoon sunlight: where we'd hit a patch of black ice and began to skip across the snow merrily as a stone over a frozen lake. Dan's face comes back to me as it had been the instant before impact: mashing the brake pedal, darting a queasy glance at me as if to say, *Sorry, babe, have this sorted in a flash.* The Volvo must have flipped onto its roof before we slammed into the tree, its hood accordioning—"Volvos are designed to crumple in zones of lesser consequence," the dealer told us.

I stand in the two-hundred-foot wake of the crash. Tufts of brown grass poke through the snow crust. Around us, the landscape unfolds in shades of igneous metal: pewter sky, sun lowering behind banks of steel-edged clouds like a Mylar balloon losing air. We're thirty miles outside Cataract City, my birthplace.

I pick up the side-view mirror, shorn off in the crash. *Objects are closer than they appear.* In its reflection I see blood weeping sluggishly from the bridge of my nose. The Leatherman took a noticeable chip out of my front tooth. The wind flays the exposed nerve endings: it's an eerie, Novocain breed of coldness.

I can feel my socked feet going numb while I shove the passenger door open against the weight of snow. I recover my boots and lace them. The keys dangle from the ignition but the Volvo isn't going anywhere and besides, an ignition spark could set any number of leaking fluids alight.

Dan's phone rests on the roof below his hanging body. The display is cracked in a thousand places; the nameless liquid of the LCD display seeps through the screen. We'd only brought along the one phone. My idea: take a sabbatical from the information superhighway. For a parent with a new child the Internet is poison. Online, every mom is doing more and caring more and sacrificing more. Online babies are cuter than your own (*it's some kind of filter,* Dan says, but I can't believe him). Online your child is never fully healthy or safe and is earmarked for some nebulous catastrophe you have no choice but to wait for.

"We're gonna be okay, Charlie."

I grab the keys, leaving him inside the car. The alarm system makes a birdlike *wheep* as the trunk folds down to spill its contents into the snow. Gas pisses from a series of pinprick holes in the trunk—the line must have ruptured. The air shimmers with fumes.

I carry Charlie to a spot thirty yards clear of the Volvo. I set his car seat under a maple to keep him out of the wind—but it's coming from all angles in bone-searching gusts. My son looks warm enough in his oversized parka. Dan and I laughed seeing it in the store, hung on an itsy-bitsy coat hanger. A pixie's snowsuit.

I haul our bags out of the trunk—my collarbone whines but the cold has a narcotic effect. What's still useable? Crushed eggs, sodden bread. Clothes saturated with gas. A sleeve of Arrowroot cookies that look okay. A rasher of uncooked bacon. We were planning on spending the night at a cabin. Dan's friend owns it—an isolated retreat, great for ice fishing or hunting if you're into that, which neither of us were.

I track around the car. The tree limb protrudes from the windshield, making the creak of a Spanish galleon rocking on the waves. The branch has pinned my husband against the driver's side window. Stubble glitters like mica on his cheeks. Long eyelashes, which he passed on to our son . . .

. . . and there is his coat, so much warmer than mine.

I'm not expecting his body to fall when I open the driver's side door. Maybe the tree sawed through his seatbelt, I don't know, but he drops untethered and his skull strikes the doorframe. Dan's body bows at an unspeakable angle. Charlie can't see this from his spot under the tree and wouldn't remember if he did. He's too young to understand that this boneless *thing* tumbling out of another metal *thing* (not that my son knows what bones are, or Volvos, or anything at all aside from craven hunger) was once the *thing* responsible for his very life.

Recently, Charlie has started to laugh in his sleep—sobbing chuckles, his lips peeled back from his whitening gums.

"What can he be laughing at?" Dan had wondered. "He doesn't know what anything is. He doesn't know what a clown is, or a banana, so he can't be laughing at a clown slipping on a banana peel."

"Would any sane person laugh at that?"

"Who says babies are sane?" he said with an arch grin before lapsing into penned-in silence. "What are the ingredients of our son's dreams, Claire?"

It doesn't matter what I do with him now. I could drag his steaming body under the tree and Charlie would only cry with hunger. But because I am his mother—filled with a mindless need to protect—I let Dan's body fall at my feet. A lock of his hair carries limply onto the toe of my boot. I unhook his feet from the pedals and stretch his legs out on the ground. He's facedown, forehead flush with the Volvo's weatherstrip. I grip his hips and turn him over, cradling his head. One eye open, one closed.

Charlie's crying. I run back to the maple, unreasonably terrified of predatory wildlife: I see talons sinking into Charlie's scalp as a massive bird carries him off, reducing my son to a thrashing dot in the twilit sky. His face is a ghastly shade of red. I wipe away the blood on his eyelids—it's partially frozen already—unzip my jacket and unsnap the nursing bra. He's fussy, rejecting me as always; my collarbone screeches when I'm forced to use my left arm to cup his skull. I shove his mouth onto my right nipple *hard*, as the lactation consultant advised. It's a bad latch but at least he settles. Charlie's got an insistent suck. Both of my nipples sport milk blisters. A few weeks ago, he spat up blood flecks like coffee grounds. I saw them on the receiving blanket. It's shocking to see blood come out of your child.

"What happened?" the triage nurse asked when Dan and I arrived in the ER. I said, "He puked out a blob of blood." Dan said: "He didn't puke anything; he *spat* up. He spits up all the time. And it wasn't a blob, it was a few dots."

It turned out to be my own blood on the blanket: I'd massaged myself trying to clear a clogged duct and burst a vessel. Charlie sucked the blood out with the milk and coughed it up again. Seeing as we share the same body for hours each day, it was difficult to discern exactly whose blood was whose.

"You can't overstate things," Dan said afterwards. "Words like *puke* and *blob*, they ... they *invoke*, Claire." He shook his head. "You can pin a tracheotomy stent in a man's throat at an accident scene and your hand won't shake. But you're scared to cut Charlie's fingernails."

You were born into dread, my son.

Dan said this one night in the witching hour, alone in Charlie's nursery, his voice clear over the monitor in our bedroom. He was right: to have a baby is to be introduced to a depthless well of worry. A dread you never could have guessed at, not in a thousand years. I'm eaten up with anxiety. Daily if not hourly I assess the colour, quantity, and frequency of Charlie's outputs. Is his pee too yellow, his fontanel too sunken? Dehydration. His shit's not a robust pumpkin-pie shade? Not getting enough hind milk. I suffer dreams where I've lost my son in familiar surround-ings. He's loose under the covers at the bottom of our bed like some pudgy ferret and I'm stabbing at him with my toes. During bath-time I'm torn between making sure his testicles are good and clean to prevent infection and not wanting to crush or somehow disfigure them.

"They're incredibly hardy organs," Dan assured me. "He'll inflict more punishment on them as a teenager than you ever will."

I can't picture Charlie as a teenager. A gulf of time and disease, poisonings, mutilations and senseless calamities separate him from that. Even Dan had nightmares about such things. *In this one dream, I'm heating a bottle in the microwave but I'm so tired that I set it for a minute instead of ten seconds . . . my bird's-eye view in the dream shows the milk bubbling to a boil but I don't see or care, and I carry it to*

Charlie, who's hunger-sobbing in his crib. The scariest part is that he drinks it, Claire. Every last drop.

While my son feeds, I focus. Broadly, I have two choices: stay or go. Who uses this road? Ice fishers. Poachers. The odd snowmobiler. It could be days before anyone comes. I should walk it out . . . or head to the cabin, though I don't know how much farther that is. Dan cut off Old Stone Road and drove maybe ten kilometres down the access road before the tree. Now we have no phone and not much food—or okay, Charlie has as much as he needs so long as I'm breathing. So long as.

His mouth slips off my nipple and his eyes hang at half-mast: classic milk coma. I rest him back in the car seat, slough off my jacket and drape it over him before returning to the car. I unzip Dan's parka. It's warm and smells of the filched cigarettes he smoked behind the garden shed, the cologne I bought for his birthday, of tree sap and blood.

I unbutton his trousers with hands that won't stop shaking—not unlike the first time I did this years ago in his dorm room, the two of us drunk on blue lagoons. But the pants are far too long; the warmth they'd provide would be cancelled out by my clumsiness if I wore them. I tug off Dan's woolen socks and double them over my own. He'd understand.

It's difficult dragging his body back inside the Volvo. I wrap a bungee cord across his chest and under his arms. It's exhausting but I'm desperate to give his body shelter.

It's nearing nightfall and there are wild animals to consider.

A month after giving birth I stuck my hand down my husband's running shorts. He'd come home from a jog with his long limbs sheathed in sweat. My top was hiked up, Charlie latched onto my tit. I'd spent more hours topless in that first month than the entirety of my adult life. Some real *National Geographic* stuff. As soon as my fingers slipped under Dan's waistband, our son's feeding took on the glottal suck of a pool filter. "He's occupied," I said, blasé. "Let's take a Euro attitude." Dan tried to pull my hand away and when I resisted he squinted at the ceiling, lips pursed, as though working through a complex physics equation. His cock was a warm gristly tube. It was like petting a sleeping Shar-Pei. "I'm sorry," he said. "Claire, he's . . . look, he's *staring* right at me." I got pissed and said some things. *I'm a hideous monster to you*, etcetera. Dan bore it with an expression of mortified acceptance— and that look jolted me out of the fear that his reluctance might somehow be permanent.

I tuck Dan's heels inside the car and shut the door. The BabyBjörn's in the trunk, along with a highway emergency kit. I pocket gauze and bandages, the Leatherman, a Maglite, the Arrowroots and two road flares. As I'm stuffing them into the pockets of Dan's parka, I feel something in one of them.

Charlie is shivering when I get back. I tear off the parka and wrap him in it while I put my own jacket back on. Then I don the Björn and tighten the straps. Charlie settles in, face resting comfortably against my chest. I readjust Dan's parka over us both and zip it to my throat, then remove what I'd found from its pocket.

"Daddy remembered your Adventuring Hat."

A nurse put the hat—which is really more a sock with a knot at the end—on Charlie's head the minute he was born, right before settling him under the warming table. Days later as we prepared to leave the maternity ward, Dan slipped it on our son's head.

"This is your Adventuring Hat, my boy. Now let's get out that door and start the adventure, because there's more to life than these four walls."

Charlie and I could wait until morning to set off—but that would mean spending the night in the Volvo with Dan's body. I hate transferring corpses to the morgue after hours: Even when they are locked in thick steel vaults you can hear the unmistakable squeaky-creaky, *plastic-y* sounds of their muscles stiffening.

I pull the zip-strip on a road flare and touch the sputtering end to the pile of sodden clothes. The gasoline ignites with a soft crumple. Flames play off the Volvo's manmade angles, beating back the dark and somehow reminding me that I'm still human.

Everything burns so fucking *fast*. When the fire goes out, I'm rocked with a despair as profound as I've ever known.

"None of this was your fault," I tell my husband's shape, prone behind the flame-smudged windows. "We'll be okay. We love you. We're coming back for you."

The Maglite throws a jittery coin on the snow as Charlie and I backtrack over the accident's path. The tire tracks are still visible but the snow eddies, obscuring them. It takes five hundred yards for my knees and elbows to loosen, synovial fluid flowing. *Oh, but isn't it nice to be out for a walk!* How many times have I bundled Charlie into the stroller with a soother socked in his mouth . . . then a hundred feet from our house he'd spit it out and kick up a banshee wail. But I'd keep walking, jaw set, muttering: "I will *not* be held prisoner in my own home, you little bastard." And if he insisted on making misery, I'd tell him a fairytale.

Once upon a time there was a liberated princess who had a great job and lots of friends and things to do. She was married to a prince who supported her dreams. Then one day for some stupid fucking reason the prince figured it would be fun to stick his wang inside the princess without a condom, then he laughed like a donkey and said, "Golly gee, we can't go making a habit of that." Nine months later a hell-beast shot out of her and ruined everything. The end.

Before falling pregnant (and that's exactly how it felt: like falling) I'd seen the same metamorphosis grip my friends. I'd watched them bloat up and rhapsodize about how joyous it would be to take a halfway decent shit. I'd stopped by these friends' homes after their precious bundle arrived to find radish-eyed zombies who cried at things of little importance while fleece-covered grubworms sucked the sanity out of them through their nipples.

Charlie's disposable diapers (which eco-mothers will tell you are an unforgivable sin) go into something called a Diaper Genie: it's a space-age disposal unit with a hinged lid and a pair of metal jaws to devour my son's dirty Pampers. They collect in elongated plastic bags that Dan calls "diaper sausages." One witching hour Dan and I sat at our bedroom window overlooking the street. Charlie wouldn't stop screaming. It was maybe three o'clock in the morning. A portal into a hellish fourth dimension was kindling on our closet door. In the acid glow of that hell-gate my husband and I observed a family of raccoons flip open our garbage bin and tug out Charlie's tube-like diaper sausage, which unspooled onto our driveway like a loop of blue plastic intestine. The raccoons clawed each diaper-parcel open to feast on our son's cold and seedy turds, their muzzles stained with his wastes. We beheld this from our bedroom window, locked in a vault of existential horror.

"Claire." Dan's voice was pure doom. "This is our fucking life now."

The winter wind snaps my pants against my shins. Charlie weighs eleven pounds but it's a bristling quicksilver weight; soon a persistent note of pain is singing between my shoulder blades. Charlie's head is pressed to my chest. These days, he's got good neck control—a key milestone. I breathe downwards to warm him . . . then stop, wondering: Is it wise to flood the parka with carbon dioxide?

Our son's birth was what you'd call complicated. The umbilical cord was wrapped around his stomach—dog on a leash. His heart rate plummeted. I was ten centimetres dilated when the emergency C-section was ordered. Charlie came out clotted in vernix, as if someone had smeared him in cottage cheese. His head was so misshapen that his Adventuring Hat rested at a skew. *Jesus*, I'd thought, *I've given birth to a banana-head.* He'd been trapped so long in the canal, his pliable skull bones had temporarily elongated. My beautiful banana-boy!

My breath escapes in ragged plumes as I turn back, searching for a last glimpse of the Volvo. Only the yawning dark peers back. The stars are rarely so visible in the city but here, beyond the reach of streetlamps and light pollution, they are distantly austere.

Charlie reaches up a plaintive hand, seeking my mouth for warmth. I suck on his fingers; they taste of sour milk. My right leg breaks through the snow crust into a pool of icy water. A gassy, swampy stink burbles up. My boot comes out clung with threads of black swamp-mush. I moan around Charlie's fingers and squint into the near distance, positive I'm starting to see things in the outer dark—shapes slinking beyond the glow of the Maglite. I know there are coyotes out here, and my uncle spied a timber wolf on last year's deer hunt. Snow scrolls across my feet; my shoelaces begin to ice over. I sing softly.

I'm bringing home my baby buh-hum-ble-beee

Whuh-won't my muh-mama buh-be suh-so p-pruh-roud of muh-me;

Oh! Ouch! It stuh-stuh-stung muh-me!

My bladder feels tight. I consider pissing myself for the momentary warmth it'd bring, but that's the definition of short-term thinking. Instead I unbutton my pants, slide them down—fearsomely cold wind races up my spine—and squat. My equilibrium fails, the world tilts on a sneaky gyre and I pitch forward onto my knees. The snow looms in front of my face; my hands sink elbows-deep. I snuffle snow up my nose and realize, with distant horror, that I can barely feel it: I'm nearly as cold inside as out. How could I have come undone from my body so fast?

I pick my way over to some trees, where the wind drops to a dead calm. I hang the Björn on a branch and leave Charlie draped in Dan's parka. The Maglite, tucked into the Björn, casts light off his chin: He looks like a tiny sideshow oracle.

I pee while my son watches, his smile all gums. For a moment, I stay squatted over the hole in the snow—the steam, although heatless, is comforting. After I'm done I re-strap Charlie and head back to the road. The Volvo's old tracks are ghostly now. No visible berm distinguishes the road from surrounding wilderness. I walk hesitantly, making frantic sweeps with the Maglite.

"We're fine, muh-my buh-baby boy . . ."

Stupid. What a stupid goddamn idea. A cabin getaway with an infant. But it was doctor's orders. When Charlie was a month old, we noticed one of his pupils was bigger than the other. The left almost fully dilated, the right a pinhole. Doctor Google forecasted grim tidings.

It's an aneurism! Encephalitis! Brain parasites! Our GP ran cursory tests to rule out the worst, but the issue of Charlie's sight remained. Was he tracking properly? Was he going blind?

We were booked for an appointment at Sick Kids hospital—it usually took months to secure a visit, so the fact that Charlie was seen on a day's notice was disturbing. Dan and I sat in a bright tiled office with children's drawings festooning the walls.

Dr. KRaFt, one read. *Thank YeW foR mi NEW eyeS. Lov KateY.*

Dan saw it and said: "Do you think there's a letter around here that reads: *Dr. Kraft, why did you take my eyes away and give them to Katey?*"

Dr. Kraft was a tall shaggy specimen who looked less like a doctor than someone who'd recently descended from the hills at the end of a cougar hunt. He affixed a steampunk-looking device onto his head: a matrix of penlights, hinged monocles and magnifying glasses.

"I'll inspect the nerve running from your son's eye to the base of his brainstem," he'd said. "To stimulate it, I'll need to use these drops." He showed us a squeeze-bottle. "The active ingredient is cocaine. You okay with that?"

"My son has now had more cocaine in his system than his father," Dan said afterwards.

The drops ballooned Charlie's pupils. Dr. Kraft aimed a concentrated beam of light into his eyes, inspecting them with lenses of differing magnification.

"I can't see anything," Dr. Kraft said. "But some maladies manifest slowly."

He suggested that Dan and I aim for neutral visual stimuli until further tests could be ordered. So: no bright colours or swiftly moving objects. Hence, the cabin: a vacant vista of whiteness for miles.

Charlie's Adventuring Hat shimmers in the moonlight. His cough is a bronchial rasp. I picture the cilia—superfine hairs studding his lungs—freezing and snapping off. A hummy stink rises out of the parka. My son has shat himself but his dignity is untroubled. I fumble out the Arrowroots. I'm not hungry myself: the cold has invaded my chest and shut down my appetite. I tear at the packet with fingers blistered by early frostbite. The cellophane rips, and cookies spill into the snow. I try to kneel while fighting a rip-curl of nausea; my boot splits the ice lurking under the snow and my foot comes down badly on the frozen earth.

I sprawl, cradling Charlie. *Hit the ground on your side,* the village crone yammers in my head. The busted ends of bone grind in my shoulder. My scream welds with the forest—it could be the screech of a night bird.

The wind slaps snow into my face but I can barely feel it. I rise onto one knee and try to stand. My left leg won't support me. I suspect the muscle has unravelled off the bone; tendons don't flex so well when they're half-frozen. I picture my Achilles tendon wadded up around my ankle like a loose tubesock. Can't find the flashlight. Ah well. Moonlight lays a path. I crawl to the nearest tree, digging around until my fingers close on a branch. Tear it up, knock the ice off.

I use the stick as a cane but move slower now. My thoughts a muddle, ideas moving through my brain at a syrupy crawl. Charlie's head lolls, eyes closed. How long since the last feed? I have absolutely *no* idea.

He's so heavy. He's a weight, Charlie. A burden. And it comes to me.

I could leave him here.

Weeks after my son's birth a black bird descended from the grey winter sky, a bird with lifeless eyes that roosted on my chest. Its talons gripped my ribs as it sunk steadily into me, making a nest of me. That bird and I hated each other, but we were wed.

"That is common and there is help for it," my GP said when I told her about the bird.

Our group met every Tuesday afternoon. Our club's leader is a fifty-something social worker with gentle eyes and a distaste for the La Leche League. There is herbal tea and a Loblaws fruit tray. Moms come and go. Some are cured, and some think they are. *This is a temporary condition,* our fearless leader is always saying.

The mom who said the words that haunt me was shabbily elegant, in a "Grey Gardens" way. She pulled an ice-coloured cardigan across her chest and hugged her elbows.

"I don't love you," she said, speaking to her infant daughter. "And I feel terrible about that—but should I? If you were to die for some unpreventable reason, I would only mourn the loss of who you might have become. Right now, all you are is a vessel holding my guilt and failure, a vessel that I am obliged to help survive based on a decision your father and I made, which we thought might fix us. You have ten fingers and ten toes, a head and a smile and—yes, you are *human*—and yet, you are also hypothetical. You could grow up to be an awful person and I am not arrogant enough to think that couldn't happen simply because you are mine. Every recognizably human desire you display other than hunger are ones I make myself feel for you in hopes that I will one day start to love you. But I don't. I don't love you, Esther. Not at all."

Her jaw hinged shut with an audible snap. She stared at us with eyes red and punishing while her jaw worked as if she was chewing gravel.

At the time it seemed a monstrous admission. But now, locked in the forest dark with the cold creeping through me, it feels less so. I could . . . hang Charlie high in a tree, maybe. Like those campers who hang their food so bears can't get at it. Hang Charlie high and warm and go get help and come back for him. Yes, why not? It makes perfect sense and then I can—

The village crone speaks.

See your son? See him suspended in the split crotch of a maple in the bright morning sunlight, his soft features sparkling with frost? See him up there, his smile so blissful?

Howling from somewhere. Wolves? No. The howling is inside my head. It comes and goes. Deal with it, Claire. *Deal.*

Walk . . . fall . . . walk . . .

Snowstorm comes out of nowhere. Obscuring whiteness. Flakes so thick and lovely—snow-globe snow. It makes me think fuzzy, silly thoughts.

Years ago, my paramedic partner and I found a long-haul trucker frozen to death in the back of his cooler truck out on Old Highway 6. He'd locked himself in his trailer somehow. By the time we responded he was a brick of flesh. He'd removed every stitch of clothing and crawled into a cardboard box of herring fillets. This behaviour was common in hypothermia deaths. The skin-surface nerves die, confusing the brain—which registers cold as hot, *intolerably* hot. This is why victims are so often found naked. They also seek tight enclosed spaces, like boxes or beneath porches; this is called "rooting" or "tunnelling" behaviour. I remember how mucous was frozen down the trucker's lips—it looked like fangs. Snot-fangs. But his expression was serene. A Mona Lisa smile.

My head tips forward. I'll rest a moment . . . there's the smell of Charlie's head. Best smell on earth. Baby-head. Bottle that smell, make a trillion bucks. Secretary, get me

Ron Popeil on the phone! I try to laugh. Can't. Jaw locked shut. But not so cold anymore. Warmth in my stomach like a cozy stove. Time a smooth polished rail. Seconds stretch inside my skull, snap off, fall into a dark pool.

Count steps. *Number one ... number two ... numba three ... numb ... numma four ...*

Worries. Count my worries, one through ten. Having a baby boy was a worry. Dan the only male I understood, and him only a bit. My own father was never much more than a pair of scrutinizing eyes at a cool distance. One day Charlie will become a stranger to me, too. "The day will come when he's a stranger to both of us," Dan assured me. "This choice of ours, Claire. It didn't come with a set of guarantees. A set of cautious hopes, at best."

I just don't want to lose my son. That's all. That's everything.

Numm ten ... nuh elben ... nuh twell ... twwwuhh ... numba ... nuh ... nmmm ...

We are freezing to death.

It jumps straight out at me, a fact. I feel no pain. Extremities are only disconnected parts—I sense them moving around me but have no bond with them. Eyelids frozen shut. I suck on my fingers—I suck the blisters right off, mouth full of bitter fluid—then rub my eyelids until they come unstuck. Nerves dead at fingertips, cold peeling them back to the roots. Wooden fingers, wooden face. But I'm sweating. I'm positive of that. I should shrug the parka off ... *no.*

Charlie.

. . . numma fizzteen . . . num . . . nnnuh . . .

Sunk knee-deep in snow. Drifts higher now. Snow-shoes . . . would be nice. Stilts. Legs two blunt tusks stabbing the snow. Will they snap off below the knee? You only get one body. Two arms, two legs. Push that body at the world. World pushes back. World wins. Keep pushing.

Put yourself somewhere warm, Claire.

That village hag again. But she speaks kindly now.

I'm in Mexico. Two years ago. A long time ago, before Prince Charming stuck his dick into the Princess and unleashed the hell-beast (*oh my Charlie I love you so much Charlie you're not a hell-beast my little Charlie . . .*). White sand beach. Cabana chair under a blue parasol.

Snow piled head-high, a white wall. Jesus Christ. Is Charlie still breathing? *Please.* Yes. But shallow. Condensation from our breath has frozen zipper shut. Can't zip parka any higher. Fingers frozen anyway. Black at the tips. Remind me of licorice pipes . . .

. . . digging now. Hands and knees. Make a little hidey-hole. A nice place to rest. Dig a hole, lay down and sleep a spell . . .

NO.

Standing again. Squinting at the wall of snow. Something half-buried . . . a cup? McDonald's cup, yes. That telltale yellow-striped straw . . . this is a *manmade* snow wall. The cup must have been tossed out the window of a car and shovelled to the roadside by the plow.

Drag our bodies up, up . . . cradle Charlie's head, but it bumps and bumps . . . so . . . sorry, baby. Mommy's so sorry.

Straddle the pile and slide down, down, down . . . spike-wave of pain . . . No, no pain. Only pressure. Pale legs of sunlight crawl over the horizon. Road empty. Charlie, peek at, try to see okay. Charlie's little ears blistered with frost. *Please.* Amazing things, baby . . . doctors nowadays . . . plastics polymers grafts resins—

In my pocket: the flare. The Leatherman.

Concentrate on these. Get your fucking mind right.

The *flare.* The *Leatherman.*

First year on the job, I attended at a scene at the Dovewood Arms. Rattiest rat-trap in the scuzziest block of Cataract City. A man and a woman had an argument. Guy went at her with a carpet knife. Woman took thirty-odd wounds—all defensive. Stomach, backs of hands, buttocks, between the ribs. I arrived to find that woman curled on the floor, clutching her infant daughter. She held onto that baby the whole time.

Our blood is the last part of us to cool. Facts you learn as a paramedic. Skin first, then organs. Blood holds our final vestiges of heat.

Instructions For Myself, Claire Edwards:

Bite down on the road flare. Peel the strip with your teeth.

Red phosphorous bubbles down my hand—burns are probably second-degree, but I can't feel them. Can't feel anything anymore. Good . . . that's probably good . . .

Unfold the Leatherman.

It takes an unbelievably long time to pull the knife attachment out. My fingernails tear painlessly from nail beds . . . slip the blade under your parka.

The barest pressure as the tip dimples my skin. Letting a little warmth out, is all . . .

I love you, Charlie. I love everything about you. The sour milk-balls that collect in your neck. The way you look at me in the morning: *I thought you'd left forever!* I love you even though saying so means I am not fully me anymore. I am only the coldest and most expedient manifestation of evolutionary theory.

. . . Leatherman slips from my hand. Parka heavy—heavy-*warm*. Wrap my arms around my waist. Holding that good warmth in. Kneel beside the road. Sky lighter now.

Bright dots hover in the dawn. The ghost lights . . .

No, wait. They are the lights of an approaching car.

Will it, Claire. Will your son to survive.

. . . The sky is clear. Visibility good. The air ambulance could lift off the helipad at the Niagara Gen and be here in five minutes—

—if, if, if . . . Invoke it. Make it so. The driver *will* see the flare. *Will* stop. *Will* have a phone and *will* call 911. A helicopter *will* come.

The lights become twins. The tick of a diesel engine. Close my eyes. Blackness constricts my throat—a nugget of pure darkness in my gorge. I see it then. A simple scene, as the most pleasing often are. I'm following a man through

29

the woods. Sun streams onto the canopy of knit branches; my arms are tinted chlorophyll-green. The man walks with the cheerful clumsiness of a puppy: stepping carelessly, wholly invested in forward motion. There's the smell of wood sap, and somewhere distant, the hollow drill-note of a woodpecker. I follow the man cautiously, a hand reaching out to check his reckless momentum—but then I pull back, because my only task is to follow. The man turns and looks over his shoulder. Vestiges of Dan and of myself in that face. He smiles and points cheerily with his chin.

I know where we're going. Follow me.

The simplest thing. And it's all I want in this world.

I creep forward on my knees (I think?) towards those landlocked stars which call out in an alarmed voice—*Jesus Christ!* they cry, *Are you okay?*—and I almost laugh because of course I'm okay, I'm the best I've ever been, I'm alive and of this earth and I'm a mother, do you understand me? A cold knot blooms in my stomach and suddenly I'm falling, swooning . . .

. . . fall backwards, Claire. Please, for Christ's sake, don't you *don't* you dare fall forward.

THE BURN

It's called a *contact entrance wound*. When the gun barrel rests flush with the skin, the propellant gases get forced to the inner tissues. The molecular imperative of those gases is to expand: when expelled, they blow the flesh surrounding the exit point open in an X—your classic "blow-out fracture."

The gun was an M1911 single-action recoil. The slug was a .45-caliber ACP, a significant upgrade from the 9 × 19 mm Parabellum load in your standard M9. The M1911 was a special dispensation to select recon force marines.

None of this would be mentioned in the file on my Veteran Employment officer's desk. He was about forty with a whitewall haircut. Small off-colored squares on his teeth led me to believe he'd recently had braces removed.

"Tango Company." He closed my file. "Wild bunch, yeah?"

"Can't really compare it, sir. I never fell in with another."

"Me? 1175th Recon, Echo Company."

"Ooh-rah."

I smiled. He did, too. A vein split his forehead. I couldn't help picturing a worm coughed up on the sidewalk after a thunderstorm.

His office was the industrial gray of a dead tooth. His desk was the same metal cube public school teachers got. Young vets occupied orange plastic chairs in the waiting room, leafing through copies of *Armed Forces Journal*.

"We got plenty of opportunities popping up at Occidental Chemical," he told me. "Analyzer techs at the chlorine refinery."

If you were a working man in Niagara Falls—Cataract City—chances are you've punched the clock at OxyChem, colloquially known as the Oxy. My father did. Mandatory showers followed each shift. They pump a nontoxic deionization solution into the water lines. Dad's hair went white at the roots. Cataract City buys more Just For Men per capita than anywhere except LA, probably.

"Anything else?"

He leaned back in his chair. I'd grown my hair out. My eyes might've appeared sunk into my head. A trick of the light, was all.

"A real push on for school bus drivers. Bit of a crisis, actually. Got to pass an eye test."

"No problem."

"Drug test."

"No problem."

"One-week training, paid. Twenty hours in class, twenty in a bus."

I liked kids more than most adults. It was a no-brainer.

───

The bus company assigned Route 347, servicing Niagara Falls High. My bus was a seventy-two-seat hognose pusher: hognose because it lacked a hood, pusher because its engine was in the rear.

Mornings I drove to the bus lot, poured a cup of coffee from the steel dispenser, and milled around with my fellow drivers. A lot of them were retirees or single parents, which ensured plenty of photo-swapping: wallet-sized kids and grandkids. There was some gentle needling, but none of the aggressive ranking-out common in the corps; when you drove a cheese wagon, dick-swinging seemed silly. We'd don reflective vests and head out of the yard, a stately yellow flotilla.

Sixty-three kids, grades nine through twelve. I navigated streets of prewar shotgun houses to pick them up. Mornings they were barely awake. Afternoons they were wired on Red Bull, jacked up on gossip. My eyes flicked to the rectangular seven-inch mirror above my head—the *riot mirror*—tracking down offenders.

"Howie Bigelow!" I knew everyone's name; the familiarity unnerved them. "Ice the lip or you're hoofing it home."

Not sure how I came to think of them as boys and girls, or communally as kids: I was only twenty-three. The other drivers did, so you fell into the habit. A few girls . . . I didn't flatter myself thinking they fantasized about macking on their bus driver, who, yeah, grew his hair long and sported a tattoo but probably seemed a knob for all that, sitting stiff in his seat like he had a walnut up his ass.

A month in, the phone rang.

"My daughter's set to ride your bus." A man's voice. "It's a particular situation. I'd like to meet you."

I drove to the address. A small house behind an industrial bakery. The sweet smell of proofing bread. My knock was answered by a thin, delicate man with a widow's peak. The darkened skin of his scalp told me he worked at the Oxy. He introduced himself as Cedric and shook my hand. Tendons stood out on his wrist. A mangling braidwork of bluish veins.

Cardboard boxes stamped ANDA MED were stacked beside the hallway closet. Panties were hung to dry on the banister. The size a five-year-old might wear. All patterned with cabbage roses. If the roses were pink, the waist- and leg-bands were pink. Orange roses, orange bands.

"She hasn't been to school in nearly two years," Cedric said. "The tumor, the operation, the recovery . . . relapse. But she wants to try."

Breanne—a terrible name; she preferred "Bree," which was only marginally better—sat at the kitchen table. Cedric had filled me in over the phone. She'd been diagnosed with a brain tumor at fifteen. A hot-red acorn on the MRI, socked tight between the parietal and occipital lobes. Chemo. Surgery. Next, a medically induced coma. She was sixteen by the time she came out of it. Full recovery seemed a real possibility. Then this. Whatever this was.

You got to figure she'd seen my look before. As if I had a fifty-pound bucket of clay and was trowelling it into the hollows of her cheeks, the shadowy pits of her eyes, shaping her into the girl she must once have been.

She stood up. Fuck me, the *effort*. Legs weak as a newborn foal's. I didn't move any closer. Wouldn't make it any easier. I could give her that, at least.

"You look like shit" were her first words to me.

"Cedric Dancey's girl?" my father said, when I told him about it. "Jesus wept. His wife couldn't hack it. She hightailed it. You can't hardly blame her. Ced . . . man's a saint. A living saint."

———

Five days after graduating high school, I was knifed outside the Mighty Taco on Pine Street.

I'd been on 4th Street: Unc's, Sharkey's, Murph's, taking advantage of the bottomless-cup specials with the border-hopping Canucks. I was swaying up Pine when some guys bumped me coming out of the taco joint. Words were exchanged, and then me and one of them squared off. I'd boxed the Golden Gloves eliminators, basement of Saint Hagop Armenian Church four blocks away. My right fist caught him in the neck. He staggered, and I pressed in, but then I saw my arm was all blood. The slash came up under my armpit halfway across my biceps.

Two things I'm thinking.

One: I used to play baseball with the guy who slashed me. Optimists' League at Reservoir Park. The Panthers, name of our team.

Two: No way am I bleeding to death outside the fucking Mighty Taco.

"Enough?" guy said to me.

"Enough," I agreed.

Two weeks later I was in a barber's chair in the marine training depot at Parris Island, hair collecting on the pea-green tiles.

My peeps were 20/30 at best, meaning I had to be fitted for bulky black-framed army issue glasses, a.k.a. BC glasses, or birth-control glasses, because you sure as fuck aren't getting any wearing those ugly-ass things. I was at the base optician when a guy came in to pick up his own pair. They blew his eyeballs up bad: two watery yolks swimming behind the convex plastic.

"What do you think," he said to me. "Sniper material?"

Billy Merryweather from Velva, North Dakota. Our

drill instructor deemed him sufficiently malnourished to be put on double rations for the duration of our thirteen-week training junket. Merryweather's temperament was at odds with the big green machine, which did not endear him to the other recruits, many of them former football line pigs with folds of well-tanned fat bunched at their shirt collars. They were prone to numb, inarticulate silences punctuated by bursts of quasi-articulate profanity. In many ways, Basic was an extension of high school: nineteen-year-olds jacked on testosterone angling for alpha-dog status, except here everyone practiced bayoneting technique at 1400 hours. Another recruit, a partially lobotomized Arkansan named Morris, took to calling him Fairyweather.

"Fairyweather," Merryweather would say. "Clever. I see what you've done, there."

One afternoon we were field-stripping our M16A2 rifles while our drill instructor hollered: "Strip it, flip it, regrip it! Some sandy motherfucker's got you deadsighted right *now!*" Merryweather dropped his magazine spring in the dust. Pretty sure that shit was *purposeful.*

The D.I. bawled: "Recruit, you earned y'self a hole"—screwing a squared-off finger into Merryweather's forehead—"right *there.*" Merryweather thumbed his glasses up the bridge of his nose and said: "Hallelujah! I've earned the gift of second sight." D.I. bitched him *heavy* and assigned two hours of quarterdeck, but you could tell he dug the kid. He saw what I saw: Merryweather may fuck the dog on drills, but when things got greasy, he'd have your ass. Even shit-kickers like Morris knew it . . . yet it only seemed to amplify their hate.

Recruits could bank on eight hours of kip, but Merryweather earned an hour of fire watch nightly. The nocturne sergeant punted him out of bed at one in the a.m. and made him walk the base perimeter—pointless, punishing gruntwork, seeing as there was nothing to protect our fellow marines against save the odd coyote. I took to committing tiny infractions—dogging it on the p.m. run, dropping my shit-on-a-shingle in mess hall—to earn fire watch, too.

One night we were hoofing the company street, sage plants crunching under our boots, when I said: "The hell you doing here? I got to ask."

"My dad robbed a 7-Eleven when I was six," he told me. "Later I asked myself: Why not a bank? But Dad was scared of banks. Not scared the way a criminal's scared of jail; scared the way a little boy's scared of the dark."

Merryweather whistled through the chink in his front teeth. The sound carried up into that pristine Carolina night. Stars of such concentrated white.

"He earned a ten year hitch in Cass County. Years later I ask him: Why? He says he did it for the jazz. Three tours in Vietnam had turned something in him. He said it's like he'd been burned. You can't really feel a thing until you've encountered that heat again. Women couldn't do it. Booze. He was chasing the burn."

At the end of Basic, graduating recruits congregated at Vic's Tavern, a scratch-ass bar in Pineland Station. The local women were tuned in to the thirteen-week cycle; they colonized the postage-stamp dance floor. Merryweather and me sat alone. Morris heated pennies with a Zippo and flicked them at Merryweather's back. I batted one out of the air casually, heard it go *ping* on the scuffed linoleum.

One girl swished her hips and raked her hands through her hair, giving the witchy woman stare to us slavering dogfaces.

"She doesn't know what she's doing," I said.

Merryweather had seen *Cool Hand Luke*, too.

"Oh, she knows *exactly* what she's doing."

A burning penny singed his neck. Next Merryweather was up, grinding the gal with the come-hither stare. She's taking off his glasses; she's trying them on. Soon Morris was up there, dwarfing Merryweather, shit-talking him, chest-to-chesting him.

Merryweather's left caught Morris in the underside of his jaw, that spot where all the nerves bunch up. Merryweather had been waiting to throw that shot, and Morris was dead surprised when it came. It unhinged Morris's knees, and Merryweather's next punch, a right, hit Morris dead-solid perfect. He went down awkward, a ship sinking into the shallows. Blood fountained out of his burst beak.

"Nobody can eat fifty aaaigs!" Merryweather screamed, grinning right at me.

Ever see one of those red-assed baboons in rut? Merryweather, in that moment. Lips skinned back from bared teeth, tendons standing out on his neck like steel cables. Like Dragline said: *Kid, you're a natural-born world shaker.*

=

Exact, considered movements. That, I think, was how she once moved. Now Bree moved—awful to say, but fuck it—like a zombie. *Lurched.*

Each morning she walked unassisted to the bus. One arm outflung, the other at her hip like it was stirring a pot of soup. Sometimes she fell, and I let her fall, and when she did it was like watching a chest of drawers pushed out a third-story window. She would roll herself over in sections, making me think of salvagers dragging a sunken ship out of the sea. She'd laugh at the sky. Scream, other times. Cedric would stand on the porch, knuckles white as hoarfrost on the rail as she hauled herself up. Unstoppable. A zombie.

"A little help?" she might ask.

"Call an ambulance?" I might say.

A scar ran laterally across her skull, ear to ear. She wore a macramé cap. Sometimes her body moved with unself-conscious grace, and you'd see an echo of the coltish creature she'd been.

"This is cruel and unusual, dude."

"Less talk, more walk."

"Fuck off. Seriously."

She sat first seat, off my right shoulder. She favored shirts she'd worn at eight: her father had packed them in the attic, never thinking. I bought us coffees, but she didn't drink hers, just held it.

"I like the warmth."

"So why am I ordering it two creams, two sugars?"

"That's how I take it."

The other kids didn't know how to act. Bree got this broad pantomime of concern.

"Ooh, girl." Stroking her hair like she's a dog or something. "You're so strong. It's just incredible."

"I do dee-*clay*ah," Bree would say in a shit eating Southern-belle accent. "Ah say, ah say yoah con soyn is plum givin' me the *vay*puhs."

It struck me that Bree may once have been an intolerable bitch. It also struck me that she may simply be exponentially smarter than everyone else, which . . . upshot's the same.

Sometimes after school she asked me to drive to the Niagara Reservation, an arrowhead of undeveloped land projecting toward the falls. I parked and stacked wooden blocks under the tires. Opened the windows.

"Love Canal's not far from here," she said one afternoon.

Years ago Hooker Chemical—the Oxy—buried twenty-something tons of toxic material in a dump site in the southeast known as the Love Canal District. They covered the drums with six feet of clay. The city kept growing. Some councilmen pressured the Hooker bigwigs to sell. The bigwigs drilled down and showed them the green death. *Fuck it*, the councilmen said. *We're hardy stock.* In came the steam shovels and jackhammers. Up burped the toxic goo. Houses still went up. Schools. Kids splashing in puddles left by ruptured chemical drums. Sounds crazy, but you got to understand Cataract City.

"They think that might be it," she said. "The doctors."

"I'm not sick."

"Effects people differently, maybe."

The cataract surged between the firs. Thundering white, a cloud formation dragged down to earth. The pressure of water hummed against our ears like wings.

If Cedric wasn't home, we'd watch television. Once, she fell asleep on the sofa, head on my shoulder. Her hair smelled a little like Permethrin P-40, the lemon-scented insect repellant I'd sprayed on my fatigues in Iraq. The suture marks in the scar on her scalp were pleated like fish gills. She woke.

"Okay, this is weird, but I got to pee. I need your help to sit."

"Okay."

I followed Bree into the bathroom. Tiny drops of dried blood on the toilet seat froze something in me. She slung her arms around my neck. She parted her legs so I could get my own between hers. One of my hands was braced behind her back, the other under her thigh—not touching, just there. When she was seated, her hands slid away slowly, under my jawbone, fingers touching over my Adam's apple.

"Unbutton my pants?"

"..."

"I'm fucking with you."

When Cedric arrived, he retrieved a Tupperware container of syringes from the fridge. They sat in chairs facing each other. Cedric kissed his thumb and pressed it to the crook of Bree's elbow when he drew the steel out.

—————

One condition of my discharge was that I attend a weekly Vets 4 Vets meeting. My failure to show could jeopardize my Celexa prescription—those purple beauties did sand down the rough edges any man can feel.

Meetings were held at Zion Lutheran Church, corner of Michigan and 10th. First-birth mayflies swarmed the exposed bulb above the basement door. The ceaseless boom of the falls carried above the trees—live here long enough, that sound is white noise.

Cinder-block steps descended into a low-ceilinged room dominated by a mural depicting a group of men (all with blond, center-parted hair) gathered by a shaft of sunlight streaming through the clouds. The Gothic type read: *By grace alone, through faith alone, because of Christ alone.*

You could fall into the habit of imagining the men at these meetings amid the zip of bullets, clatter of tanks, and the strange songs that echo in their blood. Some of them didn't look that bad. Missing a finger, maybe, or one eye gone milky white, but when they laughed it was genuine, not the sound of dried seeds rattling in a hollow gourd. One especially decrepit specimen may've helped Boer commandos fight the English.

A horseshoe of collapsible chairs ringed a plywood lectern. Cedric was there, too. He'd been a gunnery sergeant in Desert Storm. We got talking about these meetings one afternoon, after I'd dropped Bree off. He'd decided to come.

At 1900 the meeting came to order. That night's special guest was officer cadet Dennis Fekete. A brushcut man we learned was his uncle pushed him out of the rectory in a wheelchair. Fekete had green eyes and an acne rash on his forehead, likely from whatever mood enhancers and beta-blockers he was boated up on. Fekete was missing his arms and legs. His fatigue trousers were buttoned well above his waist, I suppose because without hip bones they may have slid off. The empty pant legs hung from the edge of the chair like a pair of windsocks in a dead calm. He'd cut the sleeves off his shirt ... actually, no, fuck, *he* hadn't cut them off. What's left poked through the holes: mottled pink skin stretched over a few inches of humerus bone. A Silver Star, awarded for conspicuous gallantry, was pinned at his breast.

"I'm proud to have served," he said. "If I had it to do over, I'd give it all again."

A lot of downcast eyes. We tried to picture what it must be like, living in such a redacted state. Fekete's voice was phlegmy; he might've inhaled some superheated air during the explosion that left him like that, broiling his lungs. Fekete's stumps wriggled animatedly where they jutted from his shirt-holes. His body vibrated while expressing his points, and once came precariously close to slipping off his chair, but his uncle gathered up the camouflage fabric at Fekete's shoulders and reseated him, the way you'd arrange a sack of birdseed.

"Would I go back?" he asked himself. "Damn sure. I've got unfinished business."

Everyone else thinking: *No, man, that business is done. You're finished business.*

Afterwards, nobody could shake his hand. Mainly it was awkward back-pats, even a few head-pats. Outside, the night smelled of creosote. Mist hung between the parking lot's light stanchions. Cedric sat on my truck's tailgate with a half dozen tallboys.

Cars fled past on Main, the growl of their motors swelling and receding. Men congregated by their bumpers. The hiss of beer-can pull tabs. Fekete's uncle pushed him around on a sad-ass coronation tour.

"We ought to nuke the whole Middle East," Fekete said in his phlegm-choked voice. "Turn it into a fucking parking lot."

A few guys looked away. The uncle maneuvered Fekete over to the bushes edging the lot. Fiddled with his nephew's uniform. A pressurized stream of urine arced a good three feet, splashing the tarmac.

The uncle wheeled Fekete over. Their cheeks were flushed. At least Fekete had an excuse: he couldn't have weighed more than a buck ten. Wet spots on his dangling trouser legs stirred rootless horror in me.

"Spare a drop for a wounded serviceman?" the uncle asked.

The uncle unscrewed an oversized version of a sippy cup, the kind toddlers use, and filled it with the beer Cedric gave him. He raised it to Fekete's lips.

"You going back over soon?" Fekete asked me. "I'd go, if I could. If I could give anything more, I would."

Give what, exactly, Dennis—your fucking *head*? Q: What had no arms and no legs and made you feel like a bag of shit for still having yours? A: This motherfucker.

"When you do go back, blow a few of those sandy bastards to hell for me. Tell them Dennis Fekete sent you."

Fekete had been a few years ahead of me in high school. He ran with a pack of junior-survivalist types. Paintball enthusiasts who sent away for mail-order bowie knives out of *Soldier of Fortune*. He failed the army physical twice, signed with the reserves, and caught on as a Spec 4 small-engine mechanic in Kandahar. Through the grapevine I'd heard Fekete got his arms and legs torn off driving shit to a burn pit.

At Kandahar, you pissed into "desert daisies": metal tubes dug into the sand at a 45-degree angle. Honey buckets were also typical: 55-gallon steel drums with a splash of Anotec Blue, a wood plank laid across. Full drums were hauled to a fire pit far enough away that the wind wouldn't carry back.

While driving a load of drums, Fekete ran over a dirty mine. His body got blown out the rear window, fatigues fricasseed off his ass. The recon marines who found him must have been in an unsympathetic frame of mind. They said Fekete looked like a dog turd at the beach. Of course, that hadn't been the story Dennis Fekete told.

"Got to protect what's ours," he said, picking up on some point his cow-eyed uncle had made. The wind blew his empty pant legs sideways. "Beat back the . . . the . . ."

His chin dipped to touch his Silver Star. USMC General "Perfect" Peter Pace had pinned it to Fekete's hospital gown in the base OR—your typical "pin and spin" ceremony. His uncle held the sippy cup to his lips. Fekete had gotten it as bad as he was ever going to get it—and yeah, it was bad; dead would be better—but the only way he'd ever go back is on the USO tour. If he'd had his limbs, I would've slapped him cold. I stared at Fekete's stumps, these melted birthday candles sheened with mist, wondering how long before he killed himself. How? Hold his fucking breath? His uncle could push him to the edge of a swimming pool. Or leave Dennis a few feet shy and let him wriggle to the edge like a caterpillar.

Sliding off the tailgate, I knelt before his wheelchair.

"Know something, Dennis? Your face is . . . not a scratch. Like a baby's."

I wrapped my arms around him. I cradled his head as you would an infant who doesn't yet possess the strength to control the enormous weight of his own skull. The mad thrash of his heart behind skin as insubstantial as tissue paper. I held him for too long, then reseated him in the chair. My hands remained on the stumps; the broken points of his bones hummed frantically in their sockets.

"In a way, Dennis, you were really, really fortunate."

I touched his temple, drew my finger down his cheek near his mouth. Thinking maybe he'd bite. Half hoping he'd try.

When I pulled up at Cedric's house to drop him off, he lingered in the passenger seat.

"Want to know the most brutal thing I ever saw in my stint?"

When I didn't reply, he went on.

"Wasn't in combat. We were on furlough. Thailand. That country worships elephants, yeah? But this one, a circus elephant, guess she was a trampler. Kept stepping on her handlers." He laughed. "A recidivist trampler. Six, seven tons—what's an elephant weigh? Somebody said she had an abscessed tooth, and if you'd just *fix* it, but . . . that big foot of hers coming down. Like you or me stepping on a boiled peanut. They led this elephant into the public square. Mary, was her name. *Mary.* They chain her up. Someone has a pistol with a big fat bore. He shoots her point blank. Nothing but chip a little hide off. Thing is, she didn't *do* anything. They say she was a trampler but right then she was docile as fuck. Just stood there and let this bastard shoot her square in her face. She . . . she *whined.* Didn't know an elephant could make that noise."

Cedric unrolled the window. The falls, their endless boom.

"They decide to hang her. Some guy shows up with a derrick crane. They loop a chain 'round her neck. Hoist her up. You hear the ligaments crack in her feet. They'd forgotten to unchain her legs, you know? They get her off the ground and the chain snaps. Whatever-odd tons of elephant comes crashing down. Her hips break loud as a rifle crack. This crazy jet of blood shoots out her trunk. Everyone scatters, shrieking and giggling. She sits there, whining, covered in blood and dust . . . they got a thicker chain."

We sat a while.

"Tough one, my daughter."

"Uh-huh."

"But it's a pretty common sort of tough, if you can believe it. At some point the question gets asked: How deep's your bucket? A percentage of us, we just die. The rest, there's nothing we won't . . . a body can eat itself until nothing's left but the want."

Cedric gave me a look I couldn't place. Then he was walking to the front door.

His back split down the middle. White fire ignited at the base of his spine, ripped up each vertebra and broke into bright orange wings across his shoulder blades.

The mouse, the spider, the girl. That was Iraq, basically.

Southern edge of a desert country, between the industrial hub of Al Basra and the township of Al Hartha. Wind-shaped sand hardened into spiny formations. Sweat pooling in my eye sockets. Checkpoint 86K. A cement pillbox bordering a bone-white road. That was my home for eleven months.

Trucks. Motorcycles. Bicycles. Foot traffic. We stopped everything. What's your business? What's in your satchel? Are you sympathetic to American interests? We were tollbooth operators with Kevlar vests and automatic rifles.

Days unfolded inside the checkpoint. Four perspiring cement walls. Casement windows filmed with sand. Two cots. Two marines. We played cards. Read paperback westerns. Sweated out our body weight at regular intervals. We awaited the arrival of some unknown certainty, but when it failed to materialize, we learned to exist in the shadow of its utter inevitability.

The mouse. The spider. The girl.

The mouse was a small brown mouse. It lived on its own in a nest it built in the generator housing. That a mouse would have no family I found distantly upsetting. It dashed 'round the checkpoint walls, a blur against the cinder block. Brazen, this mouse. Nosing up to my cot, chewing the jute of my rucksack straps. I'd leave MRE cornflakes near its hole. Mouse Boy, my fellow grunt took to calling me. One afternoon it ate a Froot Loop out of my palm. I could've curled my fingers around its helpless brown body.

The spider was a camel spider, also known as a desert wolf spider. Its body was the size of a man's thumb, with an engorged bell of an abdomen. Its legs were thick and furred. It was the color of deerskin and lived outside the checkpoint in a hole dug at an angle into the sand. A camel spider exiting its hole was quite a sight. Its front legs pushed up and out, then split into four. Each limb moved in its own questioning pattern, testing the air. Next they planted in the sand, and the spider pushed itself out. Watching this, it was difficult not to picture a flower coming into bloom. The spider fed on scorpions, lizards, and huge beetles called fog drinkers, owing to the fact they spread their bumpy wings against the damp breeze to gather water droplets out of the desert fog.

The girl lived in a stone dwelling two hundred yards distant with her mother, father, and younger brother. Her father herded stringy-shanked goats. We never spoke.

They were a family who lived near the checkpoint, and that was all.

The girl's eyes were a scouring blue. When she looked at you, which wasn't often, you felt your bones lighting up in phosphorescent relief.

I spent four months at Checkpoint 86K, got two weeks' furlough, another four months, another furlough, and when I returned Billy Merryweather sat in a camp chair eating MRE jambalaya. He'd shed twenty pounds, and his skin was the color of pig leather. He touched his spoon to his forehead in a half-assed salute. He still wore those BC glasses, the right lens was bisected by a milky crack.

"How you keeping up, soldier?" he said.

"Keeping on. You?"

"Monstering, baby. I'm just monstering."

He'd been stationed north, Wardiya, near the Syrian border. He'd been assigned to a city-sweeper unit: a task force that infiltrated suspected safe houses in urban centers. The hairiest duty a recon marine can draw—the sort that saw you in narrow alleys taking AK-47 fire from second-story windows. Merryweather had picked up a terrible case of psoriasis. He scratched himself until pinpricks of blood dotted his elbows. He insisted on wearing those bust-ass glasses, notching them up his nose with an exaggerated squint.

At the blistering peak of an Iraqi afternoon we'd hop in the Humvee for patrol. Sixty klicks to Checkpoint 86L and back. Merryweather manned the roof-mounted

.50- cal. We cruised past licorice bushes and burnt-out Datsuns when he'd let loose. The throaty *bumpha-bumpha* of the gun blurred out the hum of the diesel engine, while my head snapped against the headrest from the recoil and copper-jacket rounds tinkled into the cab. Bullets slammed into the ground, throwing up staggered puffs of sand like that water fountain show at the Bellagio. Merryweather revelled in the pure *waste*, I think, plugging an empty desert with five thousand bucks of Uncle Sam's lead.

"Heat check!" he'd shout. "Heat *check!*"

Little things. His head would dart to one side, as if he were tracking something: the mouse along the floor, maybe, or a fly zipping out the door—but no mouse, no fly. Other times he'd flinch as if little balls of heat lighting had popped in front of his face. He smiled for no reason and laughed in the night. His skin gave off a goatish odor.

Every morning the girl filled a bucket at the well. Merryweather . . . I don't want to say he timed it. But when his gaze settled on her, fear overtook me like a fast car on the highway—the taste of a busted-open watch battery under my tongue.

One night I awoke, and he wasn't in his cot. I found him outside, crouched near the spider's hole. It had caught a fog drinker. The night so quiet that you could hear the crack-crackle as the spider tore apart the beetle's exoskeleton.

"My father was wrong," he said. "It's not a burn. It's a spear. A concentrated spear of light. White of a star or something. You know? That white. Painful, yeah, must be, but you can't feel it. That pure white eats the pain. The air's poison, but you can breathe. It's fucking . . . it's *ambrosia*. The spear of light is your home. Spiked on it." He squinted his glasses up his nose. Moonlight reflected off the crack, cleaving one eye. "When you come off it you're pretty grateful, for sure, because humans probably aren't built to exist on that spear."

One afternoon he claimed he was pissing battery acid and begged off patrol. I drove the circuit on my own. Upon my return the mouse was dead. The day before, Merryweather had watched it eat dry oatmeal out of my hand. He chucked his helmet at the wall, scaring it away.

"What the hell's that thing going to do when you're gone?"

Now it lay outside the camel spider's hole. The mouse's head was can-openered off. Camel spiders don't inject venom: they chew you open and eat your insides.

A bootlace was duct-taped to the mouse's tail. The bootlace was knotted to a stick driven into the sand. I slid my hand into the sand and picked it up. Its head hung off its neck on a hank of fur. It weighed nothing. Its eyes were eaten out of its skull. My hand clenched reflexively. The mouse crumpled like a cellophane bag.

Inside the checkpoint Merryweather boiled an MRE

on the camp stove. I calmly unscrewed the bayonet from my M16 and went back outside.

The spider flinched down in its darkness. Digging my free hand into the sand, I stabbed into its hole. The handle thrummed slightly, the way a fishing rod does when you get a nibble. When I withdrew it, the spider was pierced. Brownish-yellow yolk streaked the blade. There's no understandable internal anatomy to spider: they're just full of *goo*, like some carnivorous bath bead. About a thousand shiny eyes were crowded into the nightmare landscape of its face: they looked like caviar, or like fly shit. It twisted itself up the blade. Its mandibles bit uselessly at the steel. Its legs jittered over the hilt to touch my fingers. Its hairs weren't bristly, as I would have thought: more like the downy hair on a baby's scalp.

I removed Merryweather's pot from the cooker and scraped the spider off the blade with my boot. It hit the flame, legs curling around the blackening nut of its abdomen. Its head exploded, kicking its body off the stove.

Merryweather hopped up, mock-frightened, and stomped on it.

"Got the little bastard! I just saved your life."

———

I drove Bree to school. Picked her up. In between, thought about her.

Sometimes I'd place my hand on her arm to help her up and feel tension radiating from her bones, or deeper than bone: her marrow, electric. Get that close to somebody, feel that tension, it's possible to believe you'll dream the same dreams that night.

Sometimes I'd think she was crazy. I mean, shithouse-rat crazy. But after a while you realized she was simply past caring. At certain depths, not caring is kissing cousin to crazy. She did care about her father—"I don't want to die on him," she said—and evinced a generalized concern for all creatures more powerless than her, but that made it a short list.

"You're a handsome fucker," she'd say. "I mean, your nose is too big, for a start, but the rest of your features salvage it. Narrowly."

"You don't look half bad yourself. You could stand to lose a few pounds."

"Plus your teeth are discolored. You drink too much coffee. That stuff accelerates the heart. Beats faster, aging you. You'll look like Larry King before you're forty."

"Coffee!" I'd holler, hitching up phantom suspenders. "Superfood or silent killer? Maryanne from Houston, you're on the line."

After school we sat on her sofa watching TV. She'd put her legs across mine. Her feet were enormous, real gunboats, the phalanges sticking out like railroad ties. Maybe it was just that the rest of her had shrunk.

"Why don't you massage those bad girls?"

"When's the last time you washed them?"

"You really are one tall drink of asshole."

I'd never massaged feet before. I suspected there was an art, and my large, callused hands were imperfect tools. I pressed my thumb to her arch and moved the pad against the taut tendons in slow circles.

"Mmmm." Bree smiled her little smile. "Like that. Just ... like ... *that.*"

What would it be to have sex with this girl? It struck me as an act requiring delicacy and control. She didn't even look like a woman. Breasts nonexistent. Hips pronounced as ears. You couldn't take her up against a wall. Couldn't get careless. Not one move, one touch, without her permission. I saw her hip bones snapping, busted ends grinding. I pictured her breastbone cracked open like a Venus flytrap to reveal the billion-trillion things that must be coring her out: in my mind they were white-as-bone fishhooks with garbage-disposal mouths. I could kiss her all over. Rough and sinewy as most parts of me were, my lips were soft. Kiss her feet. Her calves. Each rib. Her eyelids.

People would leave things on Cedric's doorstep. Flowers. Teddy bears. Bree's room was a plush menagerie. She was embarrassed by it: "I should hurry up and die to spare everyone the expense." But Cedric was often overcome. I saw him weep over a helium-balloon bouquet tethered to a stuffed pig. Eyes sheened with tears, he told me: "They care a lot, you know? They love us so, *so much.*"

One afternoon at the reservation Bree began to seize.

Her skull slammed the window, and her body fell between the seats. I placed my hands around her, the knobs of her spine hard as cat's-eye marbles, and pulled her off the floor. She threw up, the stuff milky-sweet as pablum.

I drove to the hospital. Cedric showed up soon after, though I'd never thought to call him. When it became clear nothing could be done, she was released.

I went over that night. Bree was a bit better. Cedric offered me a beer and thanked me, but his eyes were elsewhere. We watched a bad comedy. Cedric laughed more than the material merited.

Before Bree went to bed he administered her shot. He only gave her half the dose. While he helped her into bed I picked up the syringe. I pulled the plunger and touched the black rubber stopper to the tip of my tongue.

My father has worked at the Oxy since forever. He drank a lot of water. The airborne chemicals leached moisture out of his skin. When I was a kid, sometimes I'd drink from his cup. The taste was the same as the taste on that stopper.

I kicked a hole in the sand and buried the mouse.

Merryweather began to fixate on the girl.

He kept losing weight. Veins trailed like root formations down his forearms. His eyes were sunk so far into his skull you had to figure they were touching his brain. Yet he worked out fanatically. Wall squats. Chin-ups on an exposed beam. His sun-blistered skin shiny with sweat.

"Ooh *rah*," he'd say, showing too many teeth, tendons standing out on his neck.

The girl filled the water bucket. She picked fruit off a date palm. Merryweather dragged a chair over to the spot I'd kicked in the sand. He sat on top of the mouse's grave and watched her. He rubbed his hands over his knees. He may have calibrated the angle at which the sun sparkled off her eyes.

"I bet her cunt's full of sand," I may have heard him say.

One night he told me he was going over to the girl's house, for a visit.

"You can't even speak the language."

"I want to see how they live, is all."

"You can see from here."

His fists balled whitely. He put his Browning 1911 on the mattress.

"I'm not going armed."

But Merryweather always carried a knife in his boot.

I went outside to use the desert daisy. Fear thrummed in my veins, an electric impulse with no place to discharge. The evening rain had tapered to a warm drizzle. I unzipped, inserted my penis into the cold metal tube. I watched the predatory lope of a hyena beneath a low-slung moon and thought about how on Sunday mornings at the farmers' market lambs lay on folding tables, skinned, their eyes bulging nakedly. When I returned home, months later, my father will say: "No two ways with you anymore, is there? When you're happy—*bam!*—you're purest happy. I like it, though," he'd say, but his eyes would remain riveted on the rim of his beer bottle.

Her cunt's full of sand. . . .

The gunshot set the hyenas gibbering in the dunes.

=====

Cedric had sold his truck to defray Bree's sky-high medical bills. I pulled up to the bus stop outside the Oxy, offered him a ride. He smiled.

"Hey, great timing."

I drove to a bar in the east end. Dark, the pool table felt torn to ribbons. Cedric put back a shot of Rumple Minze and said, "Thanks for this." We drank Busch and watched the Colts annihilate the Bills.

Afterwards I drove to the reservation. Mine the only car in sight. Beyond the lot lights, the falls growled like a living thing.

"She's not getting any better."

"Maybe not," Cedric said. The red bands circling his eyes made it look as if his blood was eating its way into the whites. "But she's . . . can't give up hope."

"You know my father's at the Oxy, right?" I said. "The chlorine refinery."

Cedric rolled down the window and fiddled with the side view mirror, like to check if there was anyone behind us.

"Chlorine," I said. "One mean bastard of a chemical."

"We take precautions."

"Insurgents used it in Iraq," I said. "They blew up chlorine tankers in public spaces. The survivors said it smelled like pepper and pineapple."

Cedric nodded, said, "Weird," still fiddling with the mirror.

"Roll that up, Ced, will you? Cold out."

"Nice night," he said, but did it. Then he flattened his palms on the dash as if bracing for a collision.

"Thing about chlorine is," I said, "it reacts with the water in our cells. Turns them into acid, basically—poisonous little balls bouncing around inside you. But once it reacts, it's gone. *Poof*, right? Untraceable."

"I really wouldn't know."

"No, not you. I'm saying if you knew what you were doing—if you mixed the right amount of hypochlorite with, say, medicine that's actually been prescribed—you could make a real mess of somebody."

We sat a stone's throw from Love Canal. The boom of the falls seemed loud enough to loosen the fillings in my teeth.

"You do it patiently enough, Ced, I guess you could make someone sick forever."

Cedric leaned back in the seat. Looked down his chest, smiling, shaking his head. His hand went inside his jacket and came out with one of the slender little blades they use at the Oxy to slit open sacks of chemical. This one had hockey tape wound around the handle to make it grippy. He opened his fingers. It sat in his palm, a silvered slice of the moon. He seemed surprised to find it there.

I cupped my hand to the side of Cedric's skull, dug my heels into the floor mat and torqued my hips and pushed. I pushed pretty damn hard.

———

When I entered the checkpoint, Merryweather was still alive. Unless, like a fish, it was a case of his nervous system firing off one last senseless fusillade.

At the military inquest I learned the bullet had entered under his right jawbone, travelled diagonally through his tongue and mouth, piercing his soft palate and shredding his pharyngeal tonsils before it invaded his cranial vault and exited the left side of his head.

All I could tell in the moment was that the hole was a scarlet sea star.

He was on all fours, head hung between his shoulders, gun still in hand. The skin under his fingernails was purple: hydrostatic pressure had burst the blood vessels. His body slumped forward until his skull touched the floor.

At the inquest I heard Merryweather had been involved in the deaths of five Iraqis. His unit fired on a transport truck that failed to heed their warning. The truck bed was full of goat herders. Three of the five were children.

The Judge Advocate General asked me to pin down

Merryweather's frame of mind. I told him about the mouse. That I'd heard him cry at night. Just procedural i-dotting and t-crossing. Marines do eat the gun. Tragic, but it happens.

The forensics examiner said it was odd that the victim, as he called Merryweather, was still holding the gun. Apparently recoil, coupled with the force of the skull snapping back, usually causes the weapon to fly out of a victim's hand. As opposed to TV crime scenes on the shows I'd watched, in which suicides are always found holding the gun.

The examiner also said contact entry wounds are nearly nonexistent in such cases. The pathology of the victim, his typical mind-set, is he's debating his decision to the end— "Searching for the hand of God," is how the examiner put it—and at the last instant pulls the gun away or angles his head back a fraction, so the barrel isn't flush with the skin. He absorbs an intermediate wound, with soot tattoos peppering the entry hole.

I was discharged following the inquest. Apparently the pathology of a marine who witnesses a fellow marine kill himself is a marked tendency toward moodiness and social disengagement, making him of questionable benefit. I didn't gripe it. I'd had all I could stand of the big green bastard. Eat the apple. Fuck the corps.

Months later Merryweather's mother wrote me. She found my name in a notebook among his personal effects. Ten pages of small, neat cursive. She told me her son had been born premature. *Wasn't much bigger than a dinner bun*, she wrote. *The doctor held him in his cupped hands.* A target of school yard bullies. Once he came home with bubble gum squashed into his hair. It took an entire jar of Skippy to get it out. For weeks his scalp smelled of peanut butter. The military seemed so against his nature. I felt awkward, the recipient of such intimacies.

What happened to her son happened to a lot of us, I wrote back. You get lost over there, charting an alien geography so far from anything you've ever known; sometimes it gets to feeling you're on the airless mountains of Mars. That sandy motherfucker sinks roots into you. Of course, I didn't use this exact phrasing.

Your son was a good man and a good marine, Mrs. Merryweather. I loved him.

And in my way, I really had.

⎯⎯

We talked afterwards, Cedric and I. Sat at a picnic table in the cool dark of the woods.

"I need help," he said.

"You do."

"She'll get better."

"She's going to."

He rubbed the side of his head and told me he'd walk home. I said this was all between us and could stay that way, but he insisted, so I let him go.

I walked to the metal railing that ran along the basin and inhaled the clean mineral smell of the rock. Moonlight hit the spray at the base of the falls, and the atomized water projected it back, an inverted bowl of light. Night birds took flight from the cliffs. Cutting through the darkness, their white wings reminded me of tracer fire. That water tumbled at twenty-six metric tons per second. If a body gets trapped down in those lightless chambers hammered out by that immensity of water, well, it's gone. You can't send frogmen in: they would die looking. You could try draglining, but after a while skin goes soft: treble hooks pass right through, like through gelatin.

Back at my truck, I saw vandals had busted out the passenger window. I found a crumpled McDonald's bag under the seat. Scrupulously, I picked up shards of safety glass.

—————

Driving a school bus is routine. Wake up. Drive to the bus yard. Pour a cup of coffee. Smile at the wallet-sized grandkids. Don a reflective vest. Give your bus a careful once-over.

The legal term for what we transport is "precious cargo."

She's waiting on the porch. Her shirt's buttoned wrong, probably because she did it herself. Maybe she's looking a bit stricken, like she's lost something, but she's there. She's there. I crack the doors.

"Time's a-ticking."

"I'm coming, you rat bastard."

And she does. Slowly, tortuously, but yeah. That pot-stirring motion of her hand. Tendons bunched along her jaw. I can't help but smile.

Somewhere along the line I lost that measured quality. I may have forfeited the middle: that vast and subtle spectrum of emotions between the extremes. Before, if a beautiful girl fixed her gaze on me, I'd play it cool—now, why bother? If I'm bursting, it shows. I don't feel silly or weak, like I'm handing some crucial part of myself away.

She's going to fall. No, no, she's fine.

My hands rest on the wheel. A small flame pops alight above the knuckle of my pinkie finger, as if a wick's embedded in the skin. The flame touches the next knuckle, the next, each bursting into a tongue of fire. The sound they make igniting is low and satisfying. Every available oxygen molecule pressed into the service of that flame.

Whumph is the sound. *Whumph, whumph, whumph, whumph.*

ONE PURE THING

I was out of Attica two weeks when the phone rang.

"Tommy Griffin. Gene Tennis here."

"Gene. Hey." I sat up in bed, rubbed my palm over my nose and cheeks. "You caught me waking up."

"You keep yourself in shape in the hoosegow, Griff?"

My shrug must have carried down the line. "Nothing much else to do, you know?"

"How's that jumper of yours? Still silky?"

"They say the shot's the last thing to go."

"I'm coaching the Cascades. Up in Niagara Falls? Scrappy unit. Couple of intriguing kids."

I scratched behind my ear. Waited for it.

"You'll never play in the Big Show again, Griff. A damn shame."

"I earned it."

A phlegmy sound came from Gene's end. "Nothing's

stopping you from suiting up for the Cascades—setting aside sheer disinterest."

"Gene . . ."

"Robert Herren's up with us. He's out of rehab again and gets gassed walking from the bus to the gym door, but I'll round him into form."

Herren was the Spurs' lottery pick my final year in the Show. The idea back then was that I'd take him under my wing. Didn't quite pan out that way.

"Good luck to you both."

"Okay, okay, far be it from me to keep you from whatever wonders await you today . . . but take my number, will you?"

I scribbled Gene's number on a matchbook from the Chinese takeout below my apartment. The smell of candy-apple-red sweet and sour sauce drifted through the vents, reminding me of the CS gas they used at Attica. A month into my sentence this rat-assed second-storey man named Classic Jeff hopped up on a cafeteria table and started kicking trays this way and that, stomping packs of oyster crackers and plastic creamers. His legs flew around like a highland dancer's as he belted out a tragic Marv Albert impression, staring right at me.

"Tom Griffin for two! *Yesss*, and it counts!"

The nerve gas came down in a fog, hallucinogenic under the lights: the long-timers called it Purple Haze. Then the smell hit, spicy yet vinegary like the inside of a sarcophagus. The long cons splashed their undershirts with sweet tea and tugged the fabric over their noses and mouths. The rest of us went down as if someone had sunk an axe into our spines. My lungs wheezed as I thrashed on the floor, my size nineteen special-order canvas boaters drumming the tile.

A few days later Classic Jeff stopped outside my cell. His nose was in a splint and he had two black eyes: it looked like he was wearing a bandito mask.

"How'd you like that gas, Griffin?" Classic Jeff flashed a gooney bird grin. "I'm a Rockets fan. Your Spurs always crushed us in the playoffs."

———

Virgin Mary stood watch over the gym of Divine Redeemer Catholic School. White marble, four feet tall, her statue cast its beatific gaze down from its alcove next to the scoreboard.

"Tommy, as I live and breathe!"

Gene Tennis met me coming through the door. We hugged the way short dudes and tall guys tend to, with me leaning down so it didn't look like Gene was a schoolboy embracing his father. Gene was in his sixties and whippet-lean, with the darting hands of a point guard. He'd finally got me to Niagara Falls by clearing things with my parole officer and booking my flight.

Now Gene clapped his hands. "Huddle up, boys!"

I saw Dale Harris, a onetime backup shooting guard for the Clips. Dragan Radovic, a willowy Lithuanian who the Raptors took a flier on years back. Chris Munny, a stone-handed big who'd had a cup of coffee with the Nets.

"Onetime all-star," Gene said. "Defensive Player of the Year. Averaged nearly three blocks in the '99 playoffs, didn't you?" Gene looked to me for confirmation. "Tom Griffin."

I doled out a couple of awkward handshakes, got nods from the rest of the guys, and sat on the bench to lace my Nikes. It was nearly six years since I'd played any kind of organized ball. At Attica, the hardtop games in the yard got rough, pushy, sometimes *shanky*.

Gene blew a blast on his whistle. "Ready to get run to death, Griff?"

My lungs were screaming halfway through the second set of wind-sprints. I was gassed, yeah, but my body did respond: I felt as if I were taking a tool out of its box, blowing the dust off, and discovering that it still worked pretty well.

Rob Herren slunk into practice twenty minutes late and Gene jumped all over him.

"What's with this sad-ass bullshit?"

"Coach, sorry!" Herren stuck his hands in the air. "Couldn't find the keys to my rental."

I'd lost count of how many times Herren had been in and out of rehab, but just looking at him, it was clear that he still had that Omaha farm-boy strength, the kind that doesn't announce itself but you feel the moment it slams into you.

"Garbage, Herren. Call a cab."

"I will, coach. Next time."

"Suit up," Gene told him. "Join the scrimmage."

Herren grinned like a schoolboy. "Looking good, Griff," he whispered as he slunk off to the changeroom.

Gene broke us into teams. I was on the second unit, matched against Chris Munny. I'd played thousands of hours of basketball, professionally and in college and in high school, all the way back to when I was a kid on the courts down the street from my house—but I felt nervy as hell as Herren led the starters across half court. That feeling held until Munny sidled into the low post and we tangled up. Then it was like a key sliding into a lock: *snik*. The years peeled away and I was back in the one place where life made sense. The lines on the court had a comforting geometry, clean paths of navigation, and I knew how to maneuver within them.

Munny scored on the first possession on a robotic half-hook, walling me off with his hip. His team fed him again the next trip down, but I got my fingertips on the ball; Munny corralled his miss and pump-faked but I trailed him to the backboard and spiked his shot so hard that it ricocheted off the scoreboard.

Herren said, "Watch out for the Virgin, Griff!"

The starters beat us up. Radovic was the owner of a *wet* stroke. Herren still had it, too. Great balance, clean handles, an effortless ability to put his defender on roller skates and blow past for a runner in the lane or a heat-seeking pass to the corner. His jumper was as fluid as ever—it barely looked like he was trying as he pulled up on his defender with a half-smirk that said: *Son, there are levels to this.*

Funny thing was, Herren wasn't even the best player on the court.

"Who's that kid, Gene? Number three." Practice had wrapped. I sat with ice bags lashed to my knees. Even my eyelids ached.

"Zev Gibson." Gene, hoarse, sucked on a Fisherman's Friend. "Mid-second rounder from last year's draft. Might've gone higher but scouts saw red flags." Off my cocked eyebrow: "Discipline issues. Not drugs or drinking or on-court antics . . . just, hard to get through to. He got suspended twice his sophomore year, then declared for the draft."

"Where did he go to school?"

"Purdue. A Boilermaker."

"The coach there, what's his name—Ruggins? He's an old-school ass-chewer."

I could hear the kid out in the gym, getting up shots after everyone else had left. Six-six with a pterodactyl's wingspan and meathook hands. During the scrimmage we'd got matched on a switch; I tried to back him down but he stonewalled me until the double-team came.

"He's quiet," said Gene. "Hard worker. Needs to find his shot."

"Anyone working with him?"

"Who am I, Shirley Temple?"

"I mean a dedicated shooting coach, Gene."

I shut my eyes. Pain throbbed through me in moody waves.

"Griff. You're here for Herren, right? Remember that."

The incident had happened in Salt Lake City. Nothing much good happens in Salt Lake.

I was the starting power forward for the Spurs. We were on the road at the Delta Center. Game six of the Western Conference finals. The Jazz were up on us three games to two. John Stockton, the Jazz's magician-savant point guard, and power forward Karl Malone were the best tandem in the league. But we had a veteran squad. Dave Robinson patrolled the paint. Our point man Avery Johnson was every bit as scrappy as Stockton, if half as talented.

I'd drawn the Malone assignment, which meant throwing yourself in front of a wood chipper for thirty-three minutes a night. I knew all of Malone's go-to moves—Gene Tennis was an assistant coach that year, helping break down Malone's tendencies. Knowing exactly what an all-world buzz saw could do was one thing; trying to stop him quite another.

I was taller than the Mailman—Malone's nickname, because he always delivered—and blocked him four times in the first game. As I watched him slump to the sideline shaking his head, I allowed myself the foolish belief that I'd solved him.

By the time game five rolled around, it was clear I hadn't solved a damn thing. Malone had been one step ahead of me since game three. I felt as if my sneakers were gummed in tree sap; even when I knew the move was coming, Malone had enough leverage to loft his shot over my block attempt or bait me into a ticky-tack foul.

After one of those fouls, I headed dejectedly to the pine. That's when I heard it.

The words came from row six, seat 101—a fact I learned later, in the discovery documents.

I scanned the crowd, a thousand faces white as cottage cheese, until I settled on *the* face.

You hear people describe life-altering events as dream-like, and I truly did feel an eerie detachment for those fifteen or so seconds it took me to walk to the end of our bench and up those poured-concrete stairs. A security guard with a wilted mustache stepped into my path; I manoeuvred him gently to one side and went up the steps like a frictionless ribbon of oil. I was aware of a hum coming from the overlooking rows, a note that sounded like the purr of powerlines on a still winter's night.

The man was thirty-eight years old. Sold Wranglers at the Jeep dealership in Cache County. Had the squat unloved body of a high school linebacker gone to seed. His face with a pink undernote you see in some guys from the mountain states, as if the second layer of his fascia had been boiled.

"Say that again," I whispered, as if it were just him and me having a friendly chat.

Under the bill of his camouflage cap the man's expression was one of righteous defiance. Didn't I know who he was? A *fan*. A diehard who'd bought these seats with the sweat of his brow. That money paid my goddamn salary, didn't it, so it was his by-God *right* to enjoy the game any way he saw fit. If some thumb-sucking athlete couldn't take some playful ribbing, he was what? Supposed to fucking *apologize*?

Dance for me, is what the man's face said to me.

In my dreams I still see my fist rise like a missile launched from a cornfield silo, past my eyes, to connect with his chin. His eyes roll back as he falls, on his face the sleepily satisfied look of an infant with a bellyful of mother's milk; in those dreams I reach for him and my fingertips tug on his K-Way jacket, but in reality I never even thought to check his fall. His skull strikes the railing running down the aisle. His neck twists lewdly and he keeps falling until his head splits on those concrete steps.

———

We played three games over the next two weeks: Down to Greenville for a date with the Groove, east to Fayetteville for an afternoon tilt against the Patriots, north into

Virginia to face the Roanoke Dazzle. We travelled by
charter coach and stayed in highway-side hotels, buddy-
ing up two to a room. We played in arenas that hosted
cattle auctions and classic car shows; in Fayetteville we
waited while the Ringling Brothers circus shovelled up
elephant dung before our practice. No charter jet, no Four
Seasons, no private parking under the arena. I didn't miss
it, except the abundance of ice—the Cascade's trainer
always ran out and had to hightail it to the nearest Circle K
after games.

I was surprised to find how much I'd missed the rhythms
of being on a team. The idle time on the bus playing two-
dollar-limit Boo-Ray. The daily drills, feeling my ball-
playing muscles awaken from hibernation. The banter and
trash talk. Herren was a world-class shit-talker; the few
English words Radovic knew were curses, flex, or invec-
tive: *Bang-bang!* he'd yell whenever he canned a long ball,
but his Lithuanian lilt made it sound like *Bengi-bengi!*

We lost by five to Greenville but followed up with a
blowout win over the Patriots. Gene inserted me into
the starting lineup against the Dazzle, which we won in
a barnburner on timely buckets from Herren and Zev
Gibson's smothering defence.

Gene had me bunking with Herren. Off the court Rob
had a laidback surfer-dude vibe; take away his God-given
talent and he'd have been happy ragging Buicks at a car
wash. His skill rested on him as a niggling burden, like a
flower he'd been given that would bloom spectacularly

whenever he took the time to water it ... but it was just the wrong flower for him.

Some nights he'd slink into our room past midnight, stumbling. We never spoke about it. I didn't tell Gene. Herren was fresh come the morning and played hard, leading our team in scoring and assists. Plus, I knew it was pharmaceuticals, not booze, that had got Herren booted from the Show. A lot of pros drank. Ron Artest used to chug Hennessey at halftime. Jordan went through a six-pack after playoff tilts.

With ten games left in the season we were fourth in the division. On an off-day I found Zev on the court after practice.

"Your shot," I told him. "It's janky."

The kid shied a glance at me, no more than a quick flash of his eyes.

"Your body goes all switchblade, hinging at the waist when you let it fly. What percentage are you shooting from three this year?"

"Three hundred or about?"

"Liar. You're shooting three-forty and you know it. What about from the field?"

Zev faced me full-on. "You know already."

"I do. Four thirty-five. But you've got a good stroke from the charity stripe."

Zev mimed shooting a free throw, flicking his wrist on the release. He let his hands slap on his thighs. I'd seen houseplants more outgoing.

"Let me show you something."

Gene Tennis poked his head out of the sacristy to watch me toss Zev the ball.

"Shoot a three."

Zev did. *Swish.* I shagged the rock and passed it back.

"Again."

Miss. Front of the rim.

"Again."

Miss. Back iron.

"You might not feel it, but all three of those shots were different."

Zev set his hands on his hips. "What am I doing wrong?"

"Nothing unfixable. For one, you shoot pigeon-toed."

I had him shoot five more with his feet spread in a wider stance. I could tell it felt weird to him. His body was fighting it.

"You cock the ball too far behind your head, too. You're catapulting it. Got to bring your release point forward. Watch."

I shot, letting my arms follow through—the "elephant's trunk" release.

"Ball stays in front, see? Back of your hand facing your forehead. Balance, follow through. Nobody's ever showed you any of this?"

We kept at it. Zev's mechanics were tight. His shot didn't need to be rebuilt, just dialled in. I dragged out the bag of balls and fed him: first from the corners, then around the arc. The ball started going through more regularly; he drained ten in a row, the net snapping with the rotation of the ball. That sound. It's music. It's Aretha Franklin, it's Van Morrison. No better sound on earth.

"You keep listening to Butter," Gene called to Zev. "That's what we called Griff up in the Big Club, 'cause his shot's so *smooth*."

We shot for an hour. Pull-ups, turnarounds, fadeaways. Zev never asked for a break, not even for a sip of water. Outside of his shot, he had everything. He moved with power and purpose: it was clear he could bully his way to his spot and had the *oomph* to get off a shot when he got there—his hands so big I'd swear each finger had an extra joint. The kid had the earmarks of a thoroughbred . . . and if I could see that, then Gene had damn sure seen the same.

By the end, sweat was dripping off the ends of Zev's surgically tight cornrows.

"Thank you, Tom," he said. "I can feel it."

"We'll keep working on it."

"Yes."

I held my fist out for a dap. Zev came for a handshake. My fist butted his fingertips awkwardly, but Zev didn't seem to mind.

"You can call me Griff."

"Do I have to?"

"Suit yourself."

Three games to go before the playoffs, and we were at the Canton Memorial Civic Center for a tilt with the Columbus River Dragons. Our squad came out after half-time down eight. The arena had seats for 4,000 souls but less than a quarter of them were full. It was two-buck beer night. A wild time at the circus.

Herren was having an off night; his eyes were bloodshot, a fact that everyone ignored. He was still slashing for layups off the glass but his shot wasn't falling and he looked like he'd rather be in the stands downing those two-buck suds.

I started the half by pulling down an offensive rebound off a Herren brick. Radovic was open in the short corner but I slung it crosscourt to Zev, whose man was sagging off him. He was not expecting the rock and bobbled it on the catch, but still had room to get a jumper off—

Instead, he dished to Herren on a curl screen, rubbing out Herren's man so that Rob could take it to the tin on a deft Eurostep. As we retreated on dee, Herren shot me a side-eye. He knew Radovic was the pass to make.

We were down six midway through the third when I snagged a defensive rebound. Herren was calling for it but Zev was the one streaking towards the basket with a half-step on his man; I flung a baseball pass up court. Zev corralled it in those claws of his, took two steps and rose up for a no-nonsense flush.

"Nice pass," Herren said to me.

"Got lucky."

"Uh-huh."

Gene called timeout. I caught Zev coming in and cupped the back of his head. "Good catch." He gave me that clipped nod of his and shook his head loose.

In the huddle, Gene gave me a lingering look. "Play inside the scheme. Move the ball. Make the correct read."

Gene subbed Munny in, and I took a seat on the pine. I was being punished. With me out, Herren saw his regular touches. But he turned the ball over and lazed on defence; on the next possession he clanked a contested three. Zev boarded the miss and dutifully cycled it to our point guard, who worked a sloppy pick-and-pop with Herren ... another miss. Meanwhile Munny was getting brutalized on defence; Columbus pulled him away from the rim on pick and pop actions and were having a field day dropping long bombs on his ass.

We were down fourteen when Gene subbed me back in with a warning.

"Stick to the game plan, Griff."

When I cleared an offensive rebound off another Herren miss, Zev sidestepped on his man. I put the ball in his hands at waist-height, exactly where his new shooting mechanics started. He rose fluidly over his defender's helplessly outstretched arms—

Clang. Front iron.

Hustling downcourt, I grabbed Zev's jersey. "You keep shooting, understand? That's your shot."

Now if you didn't know our scheme, you wouldn't be able to tell. The River Dragons probably didn't notice. But everyone on my team knew what was happening.

Griff's trying to get the kid off.

I had a favourable matchup, plus I knew things about balance and leverage honed over a lifetime in my spiritual home: the sixteen-foot-by-fifteen-foot real estate of the key. I tracked the flightpath of the ball like an egret, knowing not only that it *would* miss, but *where*; I tussled with my man, relishing the grind of hip-on-hip and employing all my tricks—pinning his arm to his side with my butt; hooking his elbow just enough to get my fingertips on the ball and steer it into my hands. I was the big dog in this arena, and tonight the big dog was gonna eat.

Of the five offensive rebounds I pulled down in the fourth quarter, four went to Zev. He shovelled off two to Herren, but on the third he hit his defender with a power dribble—the ball slamming between his legs hard enough to shiver the parquet—and blew past; my guy came over to contest and Zev slammed into him like a meat mallet, sending 250 pounds of power forward sprawling. He missed the bunny but grabbed his own rebound and banked it in soft.

The fourth rebound I could only tap out to the three-point arc in Zev's general airspace; he came down with it and rose again without thinking. The release point was true and I watched the ball arc over my head, untroubled by gravity, knowing it was good.

We would go on to lose by ten. Didn't bother me. Sometimes wins hide inside losses.

With thirteen seconds left on the clock, I was fouled and stepped to the line for a pair of meaningless free throws. As I toed the stripe, the sound rang out in the near-empty arena.

"*Muuuuuuuuuuuurr-der-eeeeeeeeeeerrrrr.*"

The culprits were a trio of adenoidal teenagers sitting in the courtside booths strung down the sidelines: small circular tables with chairs facing the court like pervert's row at a strip club. Their table was covered in crumpled beer cups, their voices fog-horning up to the rafters.

"*Murrrrrrrrrrrr-derrrrrrrrrrr-eeeeeeeeeeeeerrrrrrrrrr.*"

The ref bounced me the ball. I shot. Airball. Their heckle took on a breathless quality. Nobody else joined in, but no one told them to stop, either.

Fuck it. I shot the second one granny-style.

Swish.

That night I poked my head into the bars around our motel and found Herren propping up a stool in George's Lounge. He saw me coming and wagged his finger.

"Here he is, ladies and germs. The ole schemer himself."

I settled onto the stool beside him. He had a boilermaker on the go and the moony grin on his puss told me it wasn't his first. Two women eyeballed him from a corner booth. Rob had the lean torso of an otter, hair so long that he tied it back before games. Sun-kissed skin and the smell of the beach on him, though we hadn't been anywhere near an ocean in weeks.

"The kid's good," Herren admitted.

"He's better than good and you know it."

Herren sipped his beer and left the foam on his upper lip as he looked over his shoulder at the girls. Tinkling laughter from their booth. I'd never had that confidence with women. *Butter* wasn't the first nickname I'd earned. That would be *The Big Stiff*. And it was true: The only place my body displayed any grace was on the court.

"He'll get his shot, Griff."

"Why should he have to wait?"

"That's how it goes."

Herren had been drafted fifth in the first round. Signed a shoe deal and was started his rookie year. Sophomore season he showed up to training camp with track marks in the elbow of his shooting arm: two or three, like a cloud of blackflies had bit him in just that one spot.

Herren helicoptered a finger at the bartender. "Another round, garcon!" He pinned me with a look. "Doesn't Zev seem a bit, I don't know, *spectrum-y*?"

"What do you mean?"

"My sister's kid is autistic. I mean *seriously*. He wears these big gun-range earphones. He's not a bad kid at all. Just . . . he'll never be typical."

"Zev plays professional basketball, Robert."

"Oh does he, *Thomas*? He lives with his mom, *Thomas*. He can't look you in the eye. Obsesses on small tasks. Griff, I'm telling you."

The late game was playing on the bar TV. Vince Carter's Raptors taking on Kobe Bryant's Lakers. Christ, that Carter could fly. To watch him was to question gravity.

"You know Colbeck's retiring after this season, right?" Herren said.

Reggie Colbeck was a defensive assistant coach up with the Big Club. I caught Herren's drift immediately: Gene must be up for Colbeck's gig. Why else would he be putting the brakes on Zev? Gene needed the kid to implement his schemes on the defensive end.

"And hey, doesn't hurt Gene to have a former Defensive Player of the Year on his squad, does it?"

On TV, Bryant hit a fadeaway over Carter. Vince got whistled for the foul and appealed to the ref, all wounded outrage. Carter was a genetic freak but Kobe would always win because Kobe was a stone-cold basketball psychopath.

"Who's your hump guy, Griff?" Herren asked suddenly.

"My who?"

Herren drained his beer and flagged the bartender for another. "Y'know, the guy who stood in your way growing up. The hump."

"Jeff Harrington, at the local YMCA," I said without hesitation. "He owned a T-shirt shop on the boardwalk. Silk-screens, tie-dye—he balled in tie-dye, too, like a

Grateful Dead roadie. Harrington played rough and didn't mind if he hurt you."

"No blood, no foul."

"How about you?"

"My pops," Herren said. "He'd come home after a shift at the mill and kick the shit out of me on our driveway hoop. I'd be lucky to score a point; he'd skunk me and laugh in my face. Sometimes he'd come home late, drunk, drag me out of bed and make me play him in my pjs and sneakers; he'd jam a knee into my spine if I tried to back him down, plant his shoulder into my stomach on a drive to the hoop. *You gotta do better than that to beat your old man,* while my poor mom cried on the porch steps." Herren jutted his jaw like a bulldog. "When I got older—twelve or so—I'd lie in bed in shorts and jersey waiting for him to come home. I'd hop out of bed wide awake and take him on. Got close a few times, too. He was drinking himself to death; sometimes he could barely stand."

"How old were you when you beat him?"

"Never did. He got sent up to Raiford. Entered into some disagreement with another washout at the bar. My dad stashed a lug wrench in his lunchbox." Herren waved a stray cocktail straw like a magician's wand. "He tapped that other fellow's noggin once, twice, then a few more times for good measure. *Abracadabra,* you're a jailbird."

Herren and I stayed to watch the Lakers win by five, although that outcome was never in doubt. The next day

Rob moved into his own room. Cost him an extra thirty bucks but you can't put a price on privacy.

———

We entered the playoffs as the third seed and drew the Revelers, winners of their last four. They were on a heater and we were banged up: Munny nursing a bad hammy and Radovic with a torn ligament in his thumb. Herren was getting the extra touches and was none too shy about shooting the ball. And Zev? That boy was fixing to go nuclear.

A week ago, he went off for twenty-eight on an array of bone-crunching drives, fadeaways, and toe-the-line threes. When he set those shoulders square to the net and the ball locked in on his XXXL mitts, he was damn near impossible to stop. Last night he put up thirty-five; Gene yanked him in the second quarter when he missed a defensive rotation while helping Herren, whose man had blown past as if Rob's feet were nailed to the floor. But the score was tight and we needed the win, so Gene ran Zev back out and let him cook. I kept feeding him on slashes and corner touches—all you can eat, son!

Just before the start of the series, the carnival had blown through town. I went down and talked to one of the carnies; for fifty bucks, he gave me a hoop from the midway's basketball game. I brought it to Divine Redeemer, unscrewed the regulation rim and put up the carny's. Then I called Zev and told him to meet me.

"Let's work," I said when he showed up.

Zev nodded, scratching between his cornrows—it was something he did a lot. Pathologically? After what Herren said, I'd started to notice stuff like that.

"This rim is a quarter-size smaller than regulation, see? It's kinda squashed, too."

"It's like an egg," said Zev.

"My high school coach made me shoot on one of these," I told him. "After, shooting on a regular net felt like tossing stones in a lake."

I pointed to my second purchase: a clear plastic bag of stuffed toys, snakes and pandas and monkeys—the carnie had sold me the whole lot for thirty bucks.

It took Zev ten minutes to make his first shot. He didn't curse or cram one through the net just to see something go down, either. He plunked shot after shot off the basket, looking at it, head cocked as if that tiny rim was a puzzle to solve. When he finally dropped a free throw—a perfect swish, as it had to be—I tossed him a stuffed snake. He put it on the bench.

"No more prizes for easy shit," I promised him.

Six hours went by. We were mostly wordless. How many shots did he put up? Two thousand, at least. Foul line extended, elbows, step-backs and crossover pull-ups and catch-and-shoot threes. He missed ninety-nine percent to start, as every shooter this side of Ray Allen would. But at the four-hour mark he started to can them more regularly. One in every ten became one in eight, then one in five. The toys began to queue up on that bench like spectators as Zev's mechanics tightened: his elbow tucking, a balanced follow-through. There was something almost inhuman to it, like watching an android fine-tune its programming parameters.

"Bucket."

This was the only word Zev spoke. A monotone exhalation every time he canned a shot: "Bucket." "Bucket." "Bucket."

By the time I told him to stop he was draining bombs from two feet past the three-point line. *Swish. Clank.* Back iron. *Swish.* Side iron. *Swish. Swish.* If I hadn't told Zev to quit, I figured I'd find him curled up on the floor in the morning with the ball as his pillow.

"Now try the regular rim."

I swear, he must've canned thirty in a row. Could . . . not . . . miss. After dropping a variety of bank shots and jumpers he worked his way around the arc, eventually stepping back nearly to half court; he came up short on a heave and stood there quizzically, as if he'd expected to not ever miss again in his life.

"There you go, son!" I went to dap him up but Zev left me hanging. "There you go!"

He put the toys in the plastic bag. I followed him into the parking lot. A car flashed its lights, and a woman unfolded herself from behind the wheel. She was a shade over six feet with the languid movements of an athlete.

Zev went over to the passenger side. The woman stared at him across the car roof.

"You got something to say to Tom?"

Zev squinted up at the light stanchion. Itched at his cornrows.

"He'd like to thank you, Tom," she prompted him. "*For . . .*"

Zev said, "Yes, Tom. I, yes . . . do really appreciate it."

"And?" his mom said.

". . . and I'd like to invite him . . . *you* . . . to dinner."

Zev squeezed into the back seat with the sack of toys. I rode shotgun with my duffel bag braced across my thighs and Zev's kneecaps poking at my back.

"I'm Lisa." She lifted her left hand off the wheel and slid it across her stomach so I could shake it while she drove.

"Where do you figure all those stuffies are going to go, mister?" she asked Zev.

"Tom gave them to me."

"That's not what I asked, was it?"

When Zev didn't answer, I said that I could take them back.

"Oh, you'd better not," Lisa warned.

She drove to a bungalow in the shadow of Cataract City's water tower. Powerlines crisscrossed a paling sky, giving off the faint hum of insects. Lisa laid out crockpot beef with mushrooms, mashed sweet potatoes, green beans, a bag of Wonderbread. Zev lined his beans on his plate and squared the ends up with his fork; he ate half a loaf of bread by stacking ten slices on a side plate, buttering one side, folding it in half and wolfing it down in two bites.

"Can I be excused?"

"Sure, baby. You don't have to ask, remember?"

Zev gave me one of his clipped soldier's nods and went out to the garage. Lisa rinsed the dishes. There were no paintings on the walls, no photos stuck to the fridge with magnets—only five or six bills addressed to Lisa-Ann Gibson.

"Thank you," she said at last, standing at the sink with her back to me.

"He's a good kid."

Lisa wiped her hands on a dishtowel hanging from the pocket of her jeans and turned to face me. There was intensity in her eyes and I sat under her stare, wondering if she might burst into tears, and what I would say if she did.

"Beer?"

"Okay."

She pulled two cans off a six-pack and popped the tabs with a butter knife. Her can lay untouched on the table. I suspected she'd only suggested the beer for my sake.

"If Gene's not going to use Zev properly, I wish he'd trade us."

"I hear you. Zev's got a lot more to give."

"I see you trying to help him out there."

"You must've played."

"Tennessee Lady Vols. Four years."

She worked the beer tab back and forth until it snapped off the can.

"We shouldn't even be here, Tom. Zev ought to be in the Show, learning under a coach who gives a damn. Our agent says Zev ought to be in China or Italy . . . but Zev's better than that." She tapped her incisors with the beer tab absentmindedly, as though she needed to give her hands something to do. "Zev's not what you might call super adaptable."

"Can I ask something about your son?"

"Depends."

"On?"

"May I ask *you* something, Tom?"

"Well, Lisa, that depends."

She placed the tab over the mouth of her beer can with outsized care, as though a lot was riding on its balance.

"Why do you feel so bad about it?"

I'd been asked this before, although the question had been framed as: *Why did you do it?* The precinct detectives in Salt Lake asked. Same with the lawyers, journalists, the scab-pickers who wrote me in prison. But the intent behind Lisa's question was different. It was as if a glass window had been set into my forehead and she could see the clockwork of my brain grinding its guilty orbits.

"I should have thought more about the people I love. My wife and daughter."

Many things can be built into one moment. Later, you might have lots of time to tease apart the strands of instinct and causation in search of catharsis or clarity, and if you do, you will find that entwined in those strands are the people and places and events that brought you to that point, guiding you to that heartbeat where everything coming before acted on everything yet to come. Human lives can be ruthlessly reduced to such moments, I think. And once they pass, we have to exist with what we've earned inside them.

"Have you seen your family since you got out?"

I feel so ugly all the time. This feeling comes to me hourly . . . by the minute, in spells. I pulled out my wallet and teased a photo from one of its sleeves.

"Is that . . . ?"

Lisa took it from me and turned it over as if the answer might be on the other side.

"Who sent it?"

"Someone who was at the funeral, but other than that . . . I was in jail. No return address, and there was nothing inside the envelope but that."

She couldn't wrench her eyes away. I understood; for a long time, I hadn't been able to wrench mine away, either.

"Who the hell jammed that ballcap on his head in the casket, do you think?"

"The camouflage one."

"Yeah, the one he was wearing that night. That's so weird."

"Which part?"

"Do I have to pick just one, Tom?"

She got up and grabbed me a second beer. I slid the photo back into my wallet.

"It took him two weeks to die," I said. "At first it looked like he'd rally, but then he had a hemorrhage. They drilled a hole in his head to relieve some of his brain pressure ... his parents took him off life support. I understood why, but ... until then I wasn't quite a murderer, you know? Selfish hope."

From the garage there came a sharp note, as if Zev had blown a pea-whistle.

"Come take a look," Lisa said.

The entire two-car garage housed a model railroad. There were sheets of plywood from which rose snow-capped mountain ranges and flat prairies, a bustling farm, an idyllic Bavarian village. Zev stood in the middle of the layout in an engineer's cap; he worked the control to send a locomotive zipping around the track.

"It's okay that Tom sees, isn't it?" Lisa asked.

"Yes, Mom," Zev said, not looking at us.

I crouched for a better look: The bark on the miniature trees. The suspenders of the Bavarian alpenhorn player painted a deep nut brown. The barn with flaking shingles, a board-fence enclosing a tiny Clydesdale bending its neck at a water trough ...

Zev's paints were lined up on the workbench, his brushes clean. Six or seven tackle boxes held various models: ascending plastic trays with tiny Bavarians, milk maids and shopkeeps and children pushing hoops.

"This is his third railway. He's a perfectionist—aren't you, my son?"

"Yes, Mom."

As I watched, the locomotive rocketed from a tunnel carved into a fibreglass mountainside across a bridge spanning a whitecapped river, its epoxy waves topped with Queen Anne's lace. Smoke puffed from the train's tinderbox as it rocketed through the village, passing meticulously painted test-pattern faces.

The three of us looked on in breathless stillness—the sense rising in me that, past the garage doors, the world was in the same state of suspended animation—until the train appeared again.

———

Get down on your knees for me like you used to.

Some of the witnesses would testify that they'd heard a slightly different wording, but that was the gist of the dead man's statement.

Twenty-six million people play the game of basketball in the United States. Internationally, that number doubles to nearly sixty million. Every year roughly a thousand players compete in the NCAA tournament. For most, this will be the last meaningful basketball they ever play. Fifty-eight of that thousand will be selected in the NBA draft. Most will bomb out of the league within two years.

Teams hold training camps in July. Twenty guys earn invites. Four will get a good solid look. Of those four, two will earn a minimum-salary contract with the Big Club. The rest are bodies thrown out to keep the scrimmages going. These guys were the best in their high schools, their counties and states and college squads. And now? Warm-blooded filler.

Four hundred players will make the NBA's opening-day roster. Every year, maybe five of these will be genera-tional talents, known to the world by their first names: Wilt, Kareem, Larry, Magic, Michael, Shaq, Kobe, Lebron. Another twenty will be perennial all-stars, 20-mil-a-year dudes possessed of some minor flaw: a slow first step, bum shooting stroke, skillet hands, for-shit coach, maybe they crack under pressure, maybe they're a headcase ... these guys will be beloved by their fanbases and live in mansions and retire to become analysts or GMs or owners of rust-belt carwash chains, but they'll never quite be *The Man*.

Then there's the rest of us. The Hardhat Guys. Glue Guys. The Enforcers and Specialists: your three-point gun-ners and defensive stoppers—any team can use those guys, just as any army platoon needs its sappers and radiomen. If you're lucky you can ride that to five years haunting the end of the bench, sweating out training camp each summer. Otherwise you're a ten-day contract guy. An injury call-up guy. A cup-of-coffee guy. You've been the best player on your team since you were five years old—and you're *still* one of the five hundred or so best players on earth.

"Tolerance threshold" is an engineering term: "The maximum allowable departure a mechanism may have from its specification, beyond which it will suffer irreparable harm." It's the rpms an engine hits the instant before its gears shred and it flings itself to pieces. The thing about humans is that we can press past those inborn thresholds—to watch a fellow human reach another gear is one of the greatest joys in sport, maybe in *life*.

But it's painful to reach your tolerance threshold, too. To feel your fingertips brush against something and know, oh shit, that's my ceiling—and it's not quite high enough.

Karl Malone was already a first-ballot Hall of Famer when we tussled in Salt Lake, but he wasn't unbeatable: Michael Jordan had torn out the beating heart of Malone's Jazz in the playoffs just the year before. And midway through game one of that series I thought: *I've got your number, Monsieur Malone.*

But can you solve the tide? You can build a seawall, but the water will push until it gets where it needs to go. That steely inhuman pressure grinds you down. So Malone wasn't taking me to the woodshed—no, instead he kept winning the small battles, the ones that happen two dozen times in any game. What coaches call "effort" plays. Which was fine, except for the fact that I was giving every damn thing I had.

And there it is. The ceiling.

I came up middle class. Always went to sleep with a full stomach, knowing my folks loved me. Never had to worry about anything except to play ball. I was an anomaly in the league, the nerdy big man; *the Professor* was another nickname, seeing as my nose was always stuck in a book. Malone grew up in the deep south, the youngest of nine to a single mom. He was put to work on a sharecropper's acreage at seven. He'd come up hard. But that was nothing to me, seeing as I'd played against, *beat*, lots of hard guys. I was cerebral: a patient spider spinning my web in the low block. But when talent comes out square, when brawn is equalized by brains, well, the ability to win comes down to ephemeral matters of heart and willpower—whose bucket goes deepest? And when you're locked in that kind of battle and it really *feels* like life and death out there on the court . . . everything that came before those breathless seconds in the trenches carries real weight.

. . . Malone hammered his shoulder into my chest on a drive and lofted a runner a half inch over my fingertips; I'd put him off balance just enough that his shot hit iron and hung above the rim. I was in the perfect position for the rebound and went up for it . . . then there was Karl, he's going up with me, then a hair's breadth *higher* than me to tip the ball through the net.

It was just one play. One of a hundred thousand in my career. But I'd lost it with a clear advantage. Malone had my number and would for as long as we ever played. And I was letting my teammates down, and they were locked in their own desperate battles. We'd lose the series and whose fault would it be?

The whistle blew for a TV timeout. I made my way to the bench, got a slap on the ass from Coach and—

Griffin! Get down on your knees for me like you used to!

I looked up at row six, seat 101 and saw a boil-faced camo-hatted Jeep salesperson, just the sort to have a white hood and noose stashed in a hatbox in his basement.

On your knees, Griffin.

At the trial, the prosecution argued that the words were an assault on my manhood. That the deceased was intimating that I did my best work on my knees. A vile insult, nobody would deny it, but professional athletes need a thick skin. They are rewarded handsomely to play a child's game. Now, can a fan spout any nastiness they'd like? Certainly not. But should a man have paid for a schoolyard taunt with his life?

The jury didn't see what I saw, though. The feral intelligence in the dead man's eyes. They couldn't know, as I knew, that it had nothing to do with my manhood—not in the way the prosecution claimed.

My people put your people on their knees, Thomas Griffin, back in a better time.

Like I said. A lot of little things get built into one moment.

D-League playoff series went best-of-five. We won the first two against the Revelers; Herren found his stroke and Zev had a monster game two: twenty points, fifteen boards, four blocks, six steals. But the Revelers hit the drawing board and stormed back to take the next two at home. It was back to Niagara Falls for a deciding game.

The morning of the game Herren skipped practice. Gene told the team he was fighting a flu bug. Back at the motel I saw a slimy specimen skulking out of Herren's room; the guy propped the door open and headed down the hall with an ice bucket.

I caught Herren's reflection in the bathroom mirror through the open door: he was leaning against the toilet in his underwear. His eyes were half-lidded when he spotted me. He licked his lips and raised one hand limply; it dangled from his wrist like a marionette's.

The seedy dude came back with some ice.

"Go," I told him.

I perched on the edge of the tub. Whatever Herren had taken made him serene. He looked genuinely happy which was rare for him, except sometimes on the court.

"How long you been back on it?"

Herren let his head loll against the toilet tank. His neck stretched taut, his Adam's apple hard as a peach stone.

"We've got a game in seven hours, Rob."

"*Yyyyy*-up."

"Do you remember the last time you really loved the game, man?"

Herren barked acid laughter. "Don't give me that cornball bullshit. You and I been around too long, Griff."

"But do you?"

"Do *you?*"

"I love it right now, this moment." And that was the truth. "It's day-to-day, but yeah."

Herren pulled his knees into his chest and wrapped his arms around his legs. "A plumber doesn't have to love his job. Ninety-percent of walking dicks out there don't love their jobs."

"You'll get popped for this, Rob. The metabolites won't wash out of your system."

"You don't think I can lay my hands on clean piss?"

Herren would play this out until he got caught, same as last time and the times before that. He knew himself well enough to realize it, too.

"We can help him tonight."

"Who?"

"Get him some early touches, get him going—"

Herren interrupted. "Can you name one underrated quality of my game?"

"I think you're properly rated all around."

He cocked his head at me. Waited me out until I said it.

"You're a leader."

"That's right, I am. You are, too. I mean that, Griff. I'd follow you into battle. I'd walk that line with you . . . and if I wasn't such a fuckup in your estimation, you'd follow me."

"I would."

"So, talking honest here: Who's going to follow him?"

He thought he knew the kid. How could he? Although I guess that was his point.

"I'll follow."

"No, Griff. You'll *lead*."

He let his eyes slip shut. "I tell you, that hoop feels big as a barrel to me. I wouldn't be surprised if I go off for fifty tonight."

I set the back of my hand on his forehead, same way you check if your kid's running a fever. "You should skip tonight's game."

When his eyes opened there was something poisonous in them.

"You got that look, Griff."

"What look's that?"

"That killer's look. I was the last guy you passed on the bench that night, remember? I saw it up close and personal."

"Right," I said softly. "See you out there tonight."

On my way out, Herren started to warble a tune.

Half a league, half a league,
Half a league onward;
All in the valley of Death
Rode the six hundred.

Rob Herren, sprawled on the shithouse floor . . . but I could hear something resolute in his voice, something that still seemed to give half a damn.

"Forward, the Light Brigade!
Charge for the guns!" he said.

Into the valley of Death
Rode the six hundred.

Heading into the third quarter, we took the floor down
by twelve. The Revelers had brought the Big Show's first-
round pick down for the game and the kid shot the damn
lights out. He scored twenty mostly effortless points in the
first half, a few of them heat-check threes with a hand in
his face. We would have been down more if it weren't for
Herren and Zev both balling out of their minds. At first,
Herren hadn't looked as if he'd make it onto the court—
he was puking noisily ten minutes before tip-off—but
once the ball went up he was slashing into the paint and
dropping beautiful teardrops over his defender. Zev was
primed to go full-on Destroyer of Worlds but with Herren
controlling the offence he wasn't getting enough touches.

The Cascade's PR guy had papered the arena—free
ticket giveaways on the local soft-rock *and* hard-rock sta-
tions—but the place was still less than half-full. We retook
the court to a smattering of golf claps. I spotted Lisa in
the second row as I stood at the scorer's bench flexing my
ankle, which I'd tweaked in the second quarter and which
was by then ballooning in my Nike.

Gene said: "I can sit you, Griff. No use turning that
ankle into crabmeat."

I waved him off but something was definitely wrong: a line of fire raced up the back of my calf, making it painful to move laterally.

Herren brought the ball up. He and I worked the pick-and-roll; Zev's man helped on Herren, leaving Zev wide open for a corner three. But Herren looked him off and dished to me in traffic—a perfect pocket pass and I had no choice but to lay it in.

"Nice finish." Herren held out his hand for a low five. When I ignored it, he cackled.

Zev got switched onto the Reveler's microwave scorer and bottled him up, taking away every inch of breathing room. We clawed back to within four, then the Revelers put up eight quick points. I grabbed a defensive rebound and brought it up myself; Herren was calling for it but I worked with Zev on a curl, rubbing out his man with a hard screen so that Zev could rise for a clean look, canning it.

"You were covered," I told Herren as we backpedalled on defence.

"Bullshit."

But he was smiling.

On the next defensive stand, I double-teamed Zev's man; Zev knocked the ball loose and galloped up the court for an easy dunk. We were down eight with four minutes to go. The Revelers called timeout.

Gene pulled me aside. "Run the offence, Griff. Herren gets first touch."

I shook my head. "It's the boy's coming out party."

"You'll spend the end of the game pulling splinters out of your ass on this bench, Tommy."

But Gene needed this win, which meant he needed me in there. Next play after the timeout Zev and I went up for an offensive rebound, and when Zev came down with it, he passed out to Herren, who dropped a long two.

"Timeout!" I yelled.

I stalked over to Zev, trying not to hobble on my ankle. I grabbed his jersey and yanked him in. He struggled as I cupped my hand around the back of his head and pulled our heads together until our foreheads touched.

"I'm out here working for you, kid. You feel it?"

Nothing.

"But you can see I'm hurting, right?"

Nothing.

"But that doesn't matter, does it, because you can do this without me—can't you?"

Unblinking. "Yes."

"You don't *need* me, do you? Me or any of us."

Unblinking. "No."

I planted both hands in his chest and pushed him as hard as I could. Zev stumbled back, nearly falling. I heard the sparse crowd give a quick collective gasp.

"Then go on, motherfucker! Get cooking! Don't make me tell your dumb ass again!"

Who you are on the court is who you are off it. It's a truism that bears out. You want to know what a man's all about? Watch him play. If he's a selfish prick in his day-to-day, odds are he'll be one with the ball in his hands. If he's a people pleaser, he'll carry that onto the court. But Zev was unknowable. That may sound cruel or maybe it's sheer ignorance—but to me, in that moment, the boy was a black box.

With less than two minutes left I found Zev cutting to the hoop; he got mugged while powering through two defenders but still got the foul and the finish. He made the freebie and now we were down five. The next play, Zev swatted a layup attempt, snared the rebound and rumbled up the court; he looked off at Herren, who was spotted up in the corner—Rob was left standing like a beggar with his hands out—and hammered it home over the Reveler's big man, who brought his elbow down on Zev's head. Flagrant foul. Zev shook off the cobwebs and calmly sank the free throw.

We found ourselves down four heading into the final minute. The Revelers were playing keep-away, trying to drain the shot clock. Herren and Zev double-teamed the point guard, who managed to squeak between the tangle of their arms and dive hard to the rim. I rolled to cover, but he was a street-baller with a flair for the dramatic and he tried to nutmeg me, dropping a pass between my legs. Thankfully, I'd pegged him for that sort of empty razzle-dazzle and got my hands on it. Herren was calling for the ball but he knew this was an empty gesture. I caught

Zev with a long baseball pass and he finished on a crafty Eurostep, drawing another foul.

Fifteen seconds to go. Revelers up one. No timeouts left for either squad.

"Foul them!" Gene was hollering. "*Foul!*"

I intentionally fouled their centre, sending him to the stripe. He made the first. When his second freebie missed, I slammed into the Reveler's power forward as we jockeyed in the paint to secure the rebound. I snared the ball and pivoted, looking for Zev—eleven seconds on the clock—but he was too far downcourt. I handed it to Herren and watched him streak towards the basket, motoring downcourt behind him as our shooters fanned out to the corners in anticipation of a pass in the event Herren can't unlock a path to the rim . . .

Seven seconds.

Herren contorted his frame around two defenders and flipped up a shot, but as soon as it left his hand I knew it was a hair off, was going to come down on the far side of the basket; I clashed with the Reveler's centre and felt the powerful cry of his body as he and I rose in front of 617 spectators (the official attendance, tagged to the score sheet I scanned after the game) who witnessed our struggle with subdued interest, or perhaps genuine pity: here were full-grown men fighting like dogs over a bone of so little worth. After the final buzzer those same onlookers would atomize into the urban grid, off to bars or back home, and by then the game would seem to them an unremarkable slog perpetrated by faceless men who would never sign shoe deals, never ride in Bentleys or see their own faces on a box of Wheaties.

As the Revelers centre and I went up together, I felt that *need* coming off him in waves—something molecular was riding on this for both of us, inexpressible but real, and to lose this small battle would be to absorb a wound that might cripple us for the rest of our lives . . . and somehow, through the fickle blessing of fate, I tipped the ball to Zev out at the arc.

Three seconds.

Zev took two hard dribbles towards the left baseline, shedding his man; the shooting guard rotated over to contest Zev's shot, the two of them meeting down in Coffin Corner—

Two seconds.

Zev gathered himself and rose. His defender rose with him. It comes down to this more often than you'd think. Two men going up. Who gets up quicker? Whose apex is that little bit higher? Zev just got the shot off.

We all watched. Somewhere, far off, the game buzzer sounded.

It was short. I had watched a million balls carom off ten thousand rims. I knew the angles of a miss and it was not gonna . . .

The ball hit the near curve of the rim and bounced straight up. Zev lofted it high to clear his defender's fingertips; the rim took the energy out of the ball and gravity carried it to the far side of the rim, where it caught iron and bounced again . . .

Zev would've made it either way. Greatness carries. None of this mattered to his trajectory.

The ball hung above the cylinder, trapped in one of two broad outcomes . . . but a host of possibilities fluttered within that moment. Days later, I'd see the photo in the local rag—page seven of the sports section, after coverage of the state tee-ball championships out in Tonawanda—and spot Herren at the top of the key wearing an expression I'd never completely riddle out, but there's something forgiving in it; behind him, Gene Tennis is crouched in a catcher's stance, surrounded by our bench players, eying the ball forever frozen above the rim. I'm boxing out under the basket for a rebound that will never drop, same as I'd been taught as a six-year-old with the Mississauga Monarchs . . . and past the endline, all alone with his tongue sticking quizzically from his mouth, there's Zev.

Ball don't lie, is what I was thinking. *Men lie. Women lie. Ball don't lie.*

When I look at that photo, I see the framing of a Renaissance painting with sinners in hell clawing out of the bowels of the earth to snatch at the heels of an innocent child trying to elude their grip . . . I see we the broken: Robert Herren and Eugene Tennis and Thomas Griffin. The world doesn't owe us the charity of bearing us from cradle to grave unbroken, and anyway, of what interest is an unbroken life? But it's hard for us who are broken to tolerate the one pure thing—its grace reminds us too keenly of our own failures. Because we were all pure once, weren't we? The first time our fathers put a ball in our hands, the grain of the grip, the black grooves running across it, the smell of leather . . . the summer rain falling on a cracked court and cooking off the heat of the day, risers of steam coming off the blacktop and the shoulders of our boyhood competitors, the ball bouncing in puddles, slick and hard to hold, the after-rain sun angling off the downtown skyscrapers as the ball's trajectory carried through that golden heavenly light, through the rusted metal mesh of an outdoor hoop—

The ball bounces on the rim, pitter-pat, skitter-scat . . . and Christ, someone tell me, will it ever drop?

THE VANISHING TWIN

You can never guess the change your life might take until that change comes. That's what Charlie says—well, Charlie says *until that change darkens your door*, which is classic Charlie-talk but anyway, that's what he says and I believe him.

The new resident showed up on the afternoon transport. They called us *residents* instead of *convicts*, same way they called the place we're locked up in a *home*— technically it was a Juvenile Custody Facility—instead of, y'know, *prison*. We had *custodians* instead of *guards*. And we slept in a *bunkdown area* instead of *cellblock*. You can bet that if there was a brochure about the place, it would make sure to point out the "natural setting" and "stimulating activities," as if it was a summer camp. But no one's letting us mosey out that gate, free and easy.

The transport van bumped back down the dirt road raising a rooster tail of dust, leaving the new resident stranded in the lot. Spindly as a sapling with freckles and carroty hair sticking up in spikes. Instead of a hand, shiny metal calipers poked from the left sleeve of his overalls. When the DC gripped his elbow to lead him towards the processing shed, the boy jerked free and stood all stiff like the custodian had stuffed a sneaky pickle up his ass.

"Easy, Jim Bob." Domino-sized teeth crowded in the new boy's mouth like they were having a fight. "You'll be shocked to discover I can walk by myself . . . as well as chew gum and carry a tune."

The new resident did a sarcastic, goofy soft-shoe routine. The toes of his boots were squashed flat like clown shoes. He saw the rest of us watching through the chainlink and gave us a chummy wave with his metal hook. "Hoo boy, I've seen more clued-in faces at a petting zoo. Kidding, my new brothers, kidding."

The pack broke apart, and we all drifted back to our spots in the yard—a yard that stretched out into a half-acre. Charlie said it was the same in zoos: by law, you had to give animals enough "habitat." If you didn't, they went batshit—fighting each other, mutilating themselves, refusing to eat, screw, or feed their offspring.

Every week the DCs put on a "Treasure Hunt": hiding balsa wood glider kits, boxes of raisins and Silly Putty eggs around the yard. But Charlie always fucked off during hunt-time.

"Zookeepers freeze fish into blocks of ice for polar bears; it tricks them into thinking they're still hunting. Are you a fucking polar bear, Hen?"

"I'm not, Char," I told him. "But who doesn't like raisins?"

Our "natural habitat" had a basketball hoop, a woodworking shed and the owlhouse. It had a soccer net, too, but that afternoon we couldn't play because Brody Brooks had kicked the ball over the fence and the DCs told us, No, we aren't shagging your stupid ball out the woods.

Charlie and I staked out a picnic table at the northern edge of the yard. A poplar tree threw down shade there on summer days. It was the nicest spot, in my opinion, except for the bench near the gate, where you could see the first cut of the forest. Our days generally had a lazy rhythm—other than chores such as trimming the yard with push mowers and bagging the confetti-like clippings, or yanking crabgrass and clover until our palms blistered. But the chores filed down our edges, which was what society said boys of our sort had. We had edges.

That afternoon, Charlie and I laid ourselves out on the picnic table. A rotten-egg stink drifted over the wall; there was a pulp mill a mile away. I daydreamed about the red-haired boy with the metal hand, wondering if other parts of him were metal, too.

After a while, Alder Coates came over. "Go away," Alder said to us. Sounded like: *G'way.*

Alder was a farm boy with hay-baling muscles. Most of the farm boys I'd met were lambs, but Alder had been kicked in the head by a horse—you could see the half-moon scar where the horseshoe had ripped his scalp open—and it had screwed with his brainwaves. He had one spazzy eyeball that bulged from its socket, jittering like an egg yolk in a fry pan.

Charlie propped himself up on his elbows, squinting in the greenish light under the tree. "Come again?"

Alder said: "Out ta here," hooking his thumb.

Charlie and I were fifteen. Twins of the fraternal kind. Charlie was the smaller, with cool green eyes and dark hair that stayed slick no matter how much he washed or fluffed it. I was a head taller, and thicker in the shoulders and legs and the butt.

"Out of the Home?" Charlie said to Alder. "Oh I'd love to, but I'm worried they won't let me. I've already asked nicely. Got any ideas?"

Now the thing you need to know with Alder was, he's ratbag-crazy. He'd crept into his family's cowshed and slashed the cows' udders with a witchblade, which I guess is some kind of sickle? When the cops asked why he'd done it, Alder said the Bessies were keeping secrets.

"Or do you mean out, like, vacate this spot?" Charlie went on. "Because that'd be an order, Alder, and unless you've been promoted to deputy DC, I don't take orders from you."

Charlie was scary-smart, way too smart for fifteen—and see, Alder had the damaged brain of a five-year-old.

You could practically watch the wires heating up inside his skull, stewing his noodle. I sat on the table's edge, legs dangling, fingers knotted at my gut. I cocked my head at Alder as if to say: *Are we going to do this over a bit of shade?*

In the Home, we fought over the smallest things, small things being all we had.

Charlie made a shushing noise, as if he were calming a rabbity horse. "Alder," he said, "can I . . . tell you something real quick?"

Alder's bottom lip was shiny with spit. Charlie said: "Lean down. I have to whisper it."

I heard the *whishwssywshwss* of Charlie's breath going into Alder's ear. And I saw Alder's flapjack-flat face tighten as the blood drained from it. His bad eye sunk into its socket as if some big pressure had sucked it right in.

Charlie leaned back. "Should I do that for you?" he said—but he said so to Alder's back, because Alder had already turned away and was walking fast across the yard.

———

When Charlie and I were fetuses, I nearly ate him. That's what the doctors said. But it was more like . . . um, absorbed?

We weren't even *people* yet; we were only sacks of goo. But what the doctors told us is that sometimes with twins, one tries to suck the other into itself. It's called "Vanishing Twin Syndrome." Sometimes that happens, and sometimes the opposite: one twin flattens the other against the womb until it goes as thin as onionskin paper. It's either an act of complete love—imagine loving someone so much that you want to suck them inside you forever—or of crazy hate. Charlie almost vanished, but I guess he really wanted to live because he fought me off.

I came out a lot bigger. Ten pounds, six ounces. Charlie was four pounds-something. And it turns out I was too big because my mom bled to death. Nobody came right out and said it, but I still heard the words. *Way to kill your mom, fat-ass.*

To me, my mom was photos in albums and the voice on an answering-machine message that my dad couldn't bring himself to erase. She'd called to tell him she was leaving work, and did he want her to pick up anything at the grocery? He'd get drunk—if there was one thing Dad was all-day good at, it was drinking—and listen to that message over and over. Then one day, her voice was gone. I think Charlie erased her. But Dad figured he must have done it himself, by accident, which made him drink even harder.

≡

Charlie and I first talked to Lazlo Boal at evening chow. He walked down the long table with the thumb of one hand hooked into his overalls, his other hand—the metal one—going *clik-clik* on the tabletop. Smiling his big-toothed smile. A real swinging dick, my dad would have said.

Lazlo peeked into the steam trays. The food was grey, as if a very specialized vampire had sucked the colour out of it.

"Mighty fine vittles," he said. "Can I ask, milady, which culinary institute you studied at? Let me guess." He pressed a finger to his lips. "Le Cordon Bleu?"

The cafeteria cook, who was about five-hundred years old and was often seen smoking over the stewpot, said, "Eat it or don't eat, I don't give a rat's ass."

Lazlo took two scoops of grey and gave the cook a curtsy. "I shall eat with gusto."

The DCs watched Lazlo in their no-expression way— "The Serengeti Gaze," Charlie called it—as he sat at the table's edge and elbowed a few extra inches for himself.

Alder Coates sat across from him. Lazlo said, "Hey, you giving me the stinkeye? Just kiddin', buddy."

I saw Charlie's brow bunch up: *This guy want to get killed, or what?* But Alder was mesmerized. Lazlo had that effect. On the surface, it didn't make sense, seeing as he wasn't big or tough. But he gave you the sense that he knew things about the world, the secret ways it worked, plus he was smart—not Charlie-smart, but maybe close to. It amazed me how many smart kids were locked up, while so many stupid kids drifted around outside the Home like dopey zeppelins.

Alder said: "Where you from?"

"Slave Lake Reservation," Lazlo said. "I'm half Ticonderoga. My father was a travelling vacuum cleaner salesman from Poughkeepsie. Knocked up my mom and vamoosed! Nine months later, I came along. Before landing here I went on a dream-quest and my spirit animal—the walrus—told me to seek my fortune in the white man's world." He slapped the table. "So I hot-wired a car and that's just what I did, Sunny Jim!"

"How'd you lose your fucking hand?"

Lazlo leaned forward, staring down the table to see who'd asked.

"What makes you think I lost it?" he said to Charlie. "My dad was a goddamn robot, man. A sophisticated replicant model created by the government." Lazlo held up his hook. "This is all natural, from his side of the family."

"You said your dad was a vacuum cleaner salesman."

"That was his *cover*, man. His means of in-fil-*trayyy*-tion. It's all very hush-hush. I could tell you, but then I'd have to kill you."

It almost sounded like a threat—except that Lazlo was smiling with his horse-teeth jabbing every which way.

"I'll count ten ways your story doesn't make sense." Charlie held up his fingers. "Number one: Robots can't have kids." He tucked his pinkie to his palm. "Number two: our government can't afford to build robot vacuum-cleaner salesmen." He tucked another finger. "Number three . . ."

Charlie named ten and when he was finished he set both fists on the table.

"Now, want to give me ten reasons I'm wrong? Oh, wait: I guess you can only give me, what, six?"

I covered my smile with my hand. Four fingers, one thumb, one hook.

Lazlo said: "I don't need my fingers to count."

Charlie's jaw tensed. This sort of bickering gave him a thrill—fighting, but without fists. And he'd finally found a decent opponent.

"Come on, Hen," he said, picking up his tray.

That night I awoke in the early hours. The bunkdown area was still. Outside the barred window, twisty ribbons of smoke from the pulp mill turned silvery in the moonlight. Alder Coates lay three rows over, his chest hitching hard, that one big eye shiny with tears. I went to him. I can't say why. My sock feet whispered over the tiles.

"S'okay, Alder," I said in a hushed voice. "You have a nightmare?"

Alder tried to blink but his eyelid never quite closed fully over that bugged-out eye. The doctor sometimes made him put medicated gauze on it to keep the eyeball moist.

"Your brother says . . . says I got three eyes, Henry. Three eyes is good luck, he says—a special gift. Gift of . . . of second . . . second—"

"*Sight*, Alder. Second sight. Speak softly. I'm right here."

"Charlie says my third eye lives behind this one." Alder touched the lid of his bad eye. "Trying to . . . to push its way out, same way your grownup tooth pushes out your milk tooths. Charlie says my third eye is red as a demon's. I'll be able to see right through folks' skin. See their hearts . . . see the thoughts swimming in their brains. See their secrets, just like Charlie sees."

Drips of sweat tracked down Alder's forehead.

"Charlie says he's gonna cut my eye open and let the third eye out. Do it with a razor blade while I'm sleeping. Like, as a favour. But I don't wanna . . . wanna *see* any of that."

"*Shshsh*, Alder. The DC's gonna come."

Alder settled, shivering. "Don't let your brother cut me. Please, Henry."

"Okay, Alder."

When I crept back under the sheets, Charlie was watching me. We always slept side-by-side. Charlie liked to say we'd once shared the same heart, before our embryo split and I tried to kill him. His eyes glittered like dark little stars. "You're such a nice person, Hen."

Charlie said this the way you'd call someone a coward or a thief. A floorwalker came by swinging his flashlight. Charlie winked at me and shut his little stars.

———

Five years ago, a hulking boy named Laird Fairchild beat Charlie up beside a frozen oxbow lake. Charlie had called him "Lard" in algebra class and Laird—who had been held back in third grade not once but twice—chased Charlie down after school and kicked him in the head with steel-toed boots, chipping a few of Charlie's teeth.

I'd been home sick with a bad stomach ache. I'd seen the doctor twice; at first he'd prescribed pills, then a chalky syrup called Cytotec. Neither worked, but months later, when Charlie and I were placed in different classes at school, the ache went away on its own.

When Charlie came home with a hole in his lip—it was tight and rubbery like the split in a superball—Dad had a shit-fit. I remember his cheeks were furry with a two-week beard. Some days, he'd still put on his old suit, the one he wore when he used to go to the office—except he'd been fired a couple of years before. He said it was because of Mom, but Mom had died a long time ago.

"Who in hell did this to you?"

Charlie said, "And what would you do about it, anyway?"

I knew exactly what Dad would do. He would drink. For a while his poison of choice was Crown Royal, and he'd give us the velvet purple sacks to hold our marbles. But when money got tight he switched to Ontario Premium, which came in a cardboard box, then to Proof Whisky, which came in the paper bag the cashier put it in.

"Goddamn it, Charlie, let me help."

Dad hunted the Fairchilds' name out of the phonebook.

"This is Dale Webster. Your boy beat holy hell out of my boy. Got a hole in his lip you could steer a Buick through. What sort a piece-a-shit are you raising, anyhow?"

I could hear the voice on the other end rise: a tea-kettle shriek that vibrated the receiver. Dad's face took on a funny look.

"Now hold on, hold your horses ... naturally I figured ... Bullying your boy?" He glanced at Charlie. "That doesn't sound like my ... Teasing him mercilessly ... ? No, I'm not buying that."

The voice on the other end changed. Gruff, booming. Fairchilds' father had come on the line.

"No, now listen, I never ... I did not say that!" Dad swallowed, as if he was holding back a big puke. "Right then, my apologies. I got off wrongheaded. No, that's not necessary. No ... okay, that's your right to say ... fine, I deserve that ... I'll talk to him, yes I will. You can set your watch on it."

Dad hung up. His hands shook.

Over the next few weeks, Charlie would take off without telling me where he was going. He often came home shivering after dark. Then, one Friday during our last class, I saw him drop a note on Laird's desk. As Laird's eyes staggered over whatever Charlie had written, huge anger collected in his shoulders and hands.

He caught Charlie at the bike racks after last bell, but Charlie squirmed free and sprinted across the soccer field. Laird paced after him in unlaced boots, unzipped parka flapping. I trailed them to the woods bordering the river, where the hillside spilled steeply down to the basin and scraggly pines poked out of the ground.

A bluff overlooked the hill and the river beyond. I watched as Charlie zig-zagged down the steep embankment, pursued by Laird. Near its foot was a ten-foot shelf of snow packed solid by the wind; below it lay sharp river rocks and brambles. I spotted a hole sunk into the snow crust—a tunnel?

Charlie looked over his shoulder, saw Laird coming and dove into the hole. Laird followed—I guess because he was stupid, and because he was too intent on the hunt to sense danger.

Later, I'd marvel over how carefully Charlie had planned it. He must have roamed up and down the river, searching for that spot. He had to have spent days digging the hole, making it extra-wide so Laird wouldn't chicken out. I imagined Charlie down that tunnel, digging as his fingers went numb. Stuck down there with barely enough room to move and only the cold light of the moon to keep him company, Charlie testing angles, figuring out where he could fit and where his pursuer could not. That hole didn't look like much. You could stand at its crumbling edge with the sunlight going thin past the toes of your boots. It was only scary once you were trapped in it.

That hole was Charlie. My brother was that hole.

I crept down the hillside. By then Laird's boots were kicking around the tunnel's gooseneck bend, way down. He was bellowing. I peeked over the shelf. Below me, Charlie had one boot off—maybe he'd untied it and let Laird grab it, just to suck him in deeper. He brushed snow off his shoulders and spotted me. His jaw went hard for a second, then he waved me down to the riverside.

When I reached him, Charlie was sitting crosslegged by the tunnel-mouth. Laird's head stuck out of it, but the rest of him was stuck inside. Charlie had dug the tunnel just big enough so that Laird—who was built like a bowling pin—could clear his shoulders as he went down, but not his hips. His arms were pinned to his sides inside the tunnel. His nose was bloody. And he was screaming.

"Shut up." Charlie's voice was calm and toneless.

But Laird kept screaming. Not for help—he must have realized nobody but Charlie could hear him—but for mercy. He was sorry, he said, so sorry; then he resumed screaming.

Charlie found a rock the size of a sparrow's egg, and winged it. It bounced off the tunnel ice and struck Laird's head with a hollow *wonk!*, which I would have found funny except for the sight of Charlie's eyes—blown-out pupils making them almost black; a magpie's eyes—and the blood quietly leaking from Laird's scalp.

"Charlie . . ." I said.

He unzipped his pants and took out his penis, shrunken by the cold. He duck-walked over to Laird, and he pissed. Urine splashed on Laird's skull, turning his hair into steaming wet ropes. It mixed with the blood and ran down to the riverside. Laird was quaking—the skin and bones on his skull *pulsing* as if it was full of bugs, and ready to split apart out of pure terror.

That's when Charlie leaned down and whispered something to Laird. I couldn't make out what he said, but I think I heard the word "puncture." It's funny how a *word* can be scary all on its own. Laird stopped screaming and went quiet.

"Charlie . . . ?" I said again.

When my brother started booting the snow to cave in the tunnel—nasty stab-like kicks that sent ice crashing down—I grabbed him. Charlie let out the choked yip of a leashed dog yanked away from a good smell. I let go, and he put his hands on his knees, glaring. Calculating, maybe, what it meant to let this go, and where it would put him and me if he didn't.

"I won't let anyone hurt us," he said. "Not hurt, not shame us neither."

"Okay, Charlie . . . thanks."

He walked away and left me with Laird. It was rough work pulling the boy out. I think he cracked a rib. But even so, when he crawled free, Laird hugged me. The pissy stink of his hair, and his big soft body sobbing against mine.

"It's okay, Laird. Charlie was just joking. He wasn't really gonna . . ."

"I can't explain it," Dr. Pelley said.

We were in the owl house: Charlie, me, the doctor. Something was the matter with the owl's eye. One was the yellow of a devil's eye marble. The other? Milky, like an Atomic Fireball after you suck it. You could still see a teensy bit of yellow; it glowed under the milkiness like a car headlight sunk in a lake.

Percy was the owl's name. She was a Great Horned Owl who had flown into an electric cattle fence along Old Stone Road, and had come to us in an eensy little cage. Her wing hung funny, like a sleeve without the arm inside.

"You're cleaning Percy's cage every day?"

Charlie said, "Yes, doctor P."

Dr. Pelley was pretty in a fragile way and always smelled of cinnamon hearts. She ran the owl house for the Humane Society. The program was called *Youths Give Back to Nature*.

"Could be an infection," she said. "A mold or airborne fungus. God, I've never seen it this bad."

The owl house was a shack with a roof of greenhouse glass. I spotted a caterpillar inching across the roof, throwing its shadow on to Charlie's face. The shelves were stocked with clay flowerpots, cocoa shells and weed killer. Some of Percy's feathers were whiter than usual. Little red marks formed a ring around her bad eye.

"Been scratching at it," the doctor said. "She'll make it worse."

I liked feeding Percy. At first I had tried to feed her grapes from the cafeteria. But Dr. Pelley said owls only eat things that move. So every morning I'd find snails on the high wall. They trooped out of the dewy grass so slowly that, if I watched them for too long, it would seem as if the *wall* was growing—pushing out of the ground, a plant made of solid concrete, taking the snails up with it.

They're just goo, Henry, Charlie would tell me. *Snot with a shell. Look at them, slug-slugging along. Where are they even going?*

I figured those snails wanted something better—the mystery on the other side. It was fun to dream about following them. But that wall was fifteen feet tall with razor wire tumbleweeding along the top—the sun glittered off the sharp bits, looking like the Wilkinson Sword blades in Dad's old razor.

Dr. Pelley wrapped a padded gauntlet around her arm and opened the cage. Percy screeched and tore at tufts of padding with her beak.

"She's absolutely terrified," the doctor said. "We should be getting set to release her, but with this eye, I just don't know how she'd do in the wild."

"So we can keep her," Charlie said.

Dr. Pelley said, "That's not the point of this project, Charles. The owls come to us hurt, and we release them when they're better. They return to their natural way of life."

"But if she's still hurt," Charlie said in his reasonable way, "then she can't go back to her natural life, can she? We can keep her."

"You can't really *keep* wild things. Either they die or they hurt their keepers."

I watched glumly as she returned Percy to the cage. More and more I was feeling like *I* might be the problem— in some terrible way I couldn't even guess, *I* was making the owl sick.

"I'll get the mouse," Charlie said.

It was a white one this time, its eyes the size of Red Ruby peewee marbles—the rarest of all. It came out of its cage squeaking and kicking, scratching at Charlie's fingers with claws soft as a baby's fingernails.

The doctor said, "Don't make sport of it, Charles. Take no joy in it."

"I'm not. I'm just making it comfortable before it dies."

"Are you?"

Charlie nodded. "Palliative measures. And my name is Charlie."

"Excuse me?"

"Charlie, not Charles."

"You don't have to stay, Henry," the doctor said. "I know it upsets you. But leave the door open, would you?"

The afternoon was bright and warm. Residents were scattered around the yard; the DCs watched us from shaded patio chairs. I followed a beam of sunshine to our picnic table. Lazlo Boal was lying on it. A big ole shiner squeezed one of his eyes shut, but I knew Lazlo wouldn't tell me who'd done it.

"Look what the cat dragged in," he said.

I saw that he'd detached his fake hand—"uncoupled" was the proper word, Lazlo had told me—to let his skin breathe. *The stump*, was what Lazlo always called it—the way you'd talk about something you owned, but that wasn't a part of you. Its nub had a dimple like the knot in a balloon or at the end of a hot-dog and it smelled spoiled-milky, like skin trapped under a cast.

"You mind picking my nose for me?" Lazlo asked. "I can't anymore."

"Use the hand you've got left."

Lazlo pretended to be upset. "Oh, I see—you won't help a disabled buddy prospect for nose-gold." He went silent, then said: "You can pick your friends and you can pick your nose, but you can't pick your friend's nose."

I wanted to ask how Lazlo had lost his hand—it seemed like the kind of secret friends would share—but I knew I'd only get one of his crazy lies. Aliens had abducted it, a pissed-off croc chomped it off in the Everglades, whatever. I walked over to the wall and pressed my ear to the cement.

"What are you doing, Henry?"

"Nothing. You'll think it's stupid."

"No, I won't."

Lazlo wasn't a tough kid. He didn't have that freaky hardness that was rooted in most of us at the Home. He didn't have the genuine craziness, either, the kind you saw in guys like Alder Coates, who only put his pants on in the morning so he could stick his hands down them. I figured I might never know exactly how Lazlo had ended up here, but it wasn't on account of him hurting anybody. Disrespecting property or authority, probably—or just being a screwball. He wasn't built for this place and I was pretty sure he knew it by now.

"I can feel Niagara Falls," I said. "When I put my ear on the wall, I feel it through the brick . . . I . . . I can't say why . . ."

Lazlo nodded, as if to say I'd explained the feeling perfectly. I pressed my whole body to the wall. A snail was stuck to it near my elbow, higher than I'd ever seen one before.

When at last I sat back down next to Lazlo, he said: "It was bloodflow. Poor bloodflow, that's all." He held up the stump. "The veins in my hand . . . they could've belonged to a ninety-year-old guy. The skin had started to die. The problem could've spread, right? The elbow, shoulder. You sacrifice a little to save the rest."

"You're serious?"

He said, "Serious," and I could tell he meant it.

Lazlo picked up the fake hand with his good hand, flipping and catching it. "I was in a ward with other people who'd lost arms and legs, boobs and even nuts. The doctors said if we talked about it, shared our *commonality of circumstance*, we'd feel better. But none of us had got anything blown off diffusing a bomb, or jumping out of an airplane on a top-secret recon mission. They'd stepped on a rusty nail or cut a finger cleaning their fucking aquarium and some fish-bacteria ate their skin. Or they'd scarfed too many Charleston Chews, got diabetes and the doctors had to cut off the sugary bits. You'd sit there listening to these stories and think, Holy shit! This is so *boring*."

He touched the calipers on his fake hand to his tongue, tasting the metal. I glanced over at the owl house to find Charlie watching us. A cold stone lodged in my gut.

"Fuck off, Lazlo, you fucking spaz."

I cocked my fist back, as if to plant it on him. Lazlo tipped back, surprised, and rolled ass-first off the table. I left him there and jogged over to Charlie.

"You guys having a happy little chat?" he said when I reached him.

"What, with the gimp? No way, Char."

That night, Charlie crawled into my bed. His body was clammy like weeping tile. He slid one arm around my chest and one under my neck and over my shoulder until his hands knit over my heart. He hooked his legs around me, digging his heels into my thighs, anchoring himself. It was spiderish: I half-expected him to sink fangs into my neck and wrap me in sticky threads. But Charlie had done the same to me in the cradle: Dad had told us how he would come into the nursery and find Charlie wrapped around me just so. One morning Dad noticed that one of my eyes was red. Charlie had squeezed me so hard that a vessel had popped. I don't remember it happening, though, or if it hurt or not. Dad could have lied about it, too.

"You think that's a black hold up there?" I whispered, pointing at the barred window towards a bruised spot in the sky.

Charlie set his chin on my shoulder and said: "Black *hold*?"

"Yeah. A place where the blackness gets held. That's why it's darker."

"They're called black *holes*, Hen, not holds."

"Yeah?"

"How could anything hold the blackness of the universe, Hen? It's *all* black, isn't it? Otherwise the sky would be white, with little specks of black where the dark is held. A black hole is a dead sun. Those stars up there? Suns. They all have planets floating around them, same way we float round our sun. But suns run out of gas. Takes a bazillion years but they do, and when it happens they die. Except a sun, like, *eats itself.* Turns inside-out. Goes from giving off light and warmth to giving nothing at all. Just a big black mouth sucking everything into it, right? It eats planets. Crushes them like a garbage compactor. It even eats the *light*, Hen. Imagine blackness so deep and hungry that it can do that."

"Weird."

"I love you, Hen." Squeezing me. *Tight.*

"Love you, Char."

Later the floorwalker found Charlie and hauled him off me. Charlie hissed and struck out with his fists. The DCs clamped him down. He spent the next three days in Time Out. Which was fine by him—Charlie doesn't feel time the same way the rest of the world does, anyway.

Copper sulfate is a mean-ass chemical. Has the look of table salt, only blue. Eats through things slowly but endlessly like an itch you can't get rid of.

Dad killed our neighbour's tree with the stuff, and Charlie helped. The tree's branches had risen over the fence, and were dropping crabapples in our yard. Dad asked our neighbour to prune it. The neighbour said no. Dad said, "Well, I asked nice."

They did it at after dark, as I watched at the window. It was the night of the first frost: the moon lit the grass with an icy glow. Two shapes stole across the fenceline, Dad with a hacksaw, Charlie with a pair of paintbrushes. Dad gashed the tree with the saw. The two of them spat on the paintbrushes and dipped them into a pot of sulfate. They painted the gashes with poison and came home, eyes blazing with their devilry.

Soon gravity began to treat the tree differently than before—punishing it, it seemed; pushing it hard to the earth. I took a bite of one of its apples and . . . well, I remembered how I'd once found a D-cell battery in the garage, busted open and furred with green acid. Curious, I'd touched my tongue to it—and the apple tasted a lot like that battery.

They say Dad's stomach was eaten all to hell by the same stuff. His intestines, too. A surgeon sliced him open and tugged out, like, fifteen feet of tubing. It was *riddled* with holes. I've read that intestines are pretty durable—stronger than plain old skin or muscle. But then again, that copper sulphate ate a *tree* to death.

Somehow, Dad was drinking it—that was everyone's best guess, anyway. Little specks—"trace residue," the cops called it—were found inside his Proof Whisky bottles. The forensic team barely noticed it at first—until they found it other places, too. Dad's shampoo bottle. His foot powder. Everything he touched or put on.

Dad was in pretty bad shape even before the sulfate. Around that time a Children's Aid worker had shown up at the house. The week before, Dad had dragged me to the animal shelter to pick up a dog. Dad's eyes were radishy and bloodshot, and the woman at the shelter not only refused to let him have the dog he'd picked out—an old, sick-looking beagle—she said she didn't think Dad could be trusted to keep a goldfish alive. Dad got pissed and pointed at me— as if the fact that I was breathing proved her wrong.

The Children's Aid worker's report said that if Dad didn't pull his shit together, Charlie and I would go into care. But by that time, there wasn't much of anything left of Dad to pull together.

The idea of being taken away scared me, but it scared Charlie even more—the social worker said there was a good chance we'd be separated. That happened a lot, she said, because foster families could only take one kid into their homes.

After that, Dad got sick. One afternoon I found him throwing up in the toilet, and what I saw in the bowl was red and pulpy.

"What the heck have I been eating?" he said, speaking into the john. Fear seemed to be cooking off his bones, hot as flames in a firepit.

Next thing we knew, he was in the hospital with a surgeon cutting his guts apart. Sure, he was a shitty dad, but he was the only dad I'd ever have and I loved him. At first, the doctors figured it was the booze. But they took some tests that led to more tests, and then the cops went to our house and found poison in everything.

A cruiser took Charlie and me to the station. Two cops, one short and one tall, sat us down.

"It's odd," the short one said.

"Odd as a cod," said the tall one.

"We got this guy, your pops," the short one said, "nearly dead from swallowing tree killer. I mean, *poisoned*, but real slow—"

"*Crafty*," the tall one said.

"Crafty, that's the word. And the question that needs asking is: Who would poison your dad?"

Charlie said: "People are always saying they understand."

The tall one said: "Understand?"

"Why Dad drinks," Charlie said. "Because of Mom, right? It wrecked him, they say, and so, like, it's okay that he is how he is. But we lost her, too."

The short one said: "You want to tell us something, son?"

Charlie leaned down to the tape recorder, and said: "We did it." Just like that.

I'd never seen Charlie more worried than he was in the moments before I spoke.

"I knew about it," I said at last.

And after enough time went by it felt like I really *had*—my mind accepted the idea that I'd done it all with Charlie.

After the trial, they let me go see Dad. He was on the sixth floor of the Niagara General. Outside his window I saw the moon hanging above the Falls—you could see the craters on the moon's surface, the rind of an albino orange. Dad had blankets pulled up to his neck in bed. Whatever lay underneath was like driftwood blown into a loose pile by the wind. The doctors had to flush his insides with sodium citrate twice a day to stop the sulfate from eating him. He had hardly any teeth—he'd thrown up so much that the stomach acids ate them down to nubs. His mouth had the look of a caved-in mineshaft.

"I'm sorry, Dad," I said.

He didn't say anything and I wondered if he was asleep with his eyes open. Then his hand snaked from under the sheets and grabbed my wrist.

"Charlie . . ." Dad's breath reeked of bitter lemon from the citrate. "Charlie is . . . *chaos*."

Dad's still alive. I sort of wish he'd die. I think he'd like that. But bodies are stubborn.

After they took Lazlo to the hospital, I found Charlie in the owl house.

It was twilight. Charlie was alone. The DCs hadn't seen him slip away but he's good at vanishing into blind spots—most of Charlie's life has been spent in that little grey slit at the edge of your vision where your eyes aren't properly focused.

There had been something wrong with Lazlo's ear. I'd overheard him complaining to the DCs that morning—which was odd, because Lazlo wasn't a bellyacher. Then at lunch he'd fallen to the cafeteria floor, shrieking and clutching his head. The DCs took him to the infirmary, but his screams carried back into the cafeteria. I had glanced at Charlie. His face was unreadable.

We had pudding for dessert. It is served in metal tins. I'd licked my lid clean, bent it in half, and when nobody was looking I slipped it into my pocket.

I lingered outside the owl house. Inside, everything was dark and still. Only the eerie rustling of feathers.

Phtooo!

Listen, it's not as if I was born nice. I'd done my share of rotten-ass stuff. I put a tack on my teacher's chair; I fed a frog Alka Seltzer to see if it would blow up like a grenade. I'd done those things and I'd do them again, or things very much like it. My father hadn't raised any saints.

And Charlie's never done *any* of those stupidly terrible things we other boys do. Every act of cruelty Charlie's ever committed had a reason. He's never been fickle with his cruelties. Everything comes from a place of strong purpose. Follow the threads back and you'll see that.

Still, Charlie's half-devil. Three-quarters maybe. He's my brother so I can say so.

Phtooo!

Percy screeched. Charlie's voice, soft and mothering in the dark: "Shshsh . . . pretty bird."

Sometimes Charlie would bring it up—the fact that I had tried to eat him. It pissed me off. Worse than that . . . it shamed me. Because with him I'd share anything. The way I saw it, we were partners. And as brothers, as *twins,* we were blood-partners.

I could see Charlie in the owl house. The nose-watering smell of bleach. He was right up against Percy's cage. Something was sticking out of his mouth . . . a straw?

Phtooo!

A white blob shot into the cage, hitting Percy. The owl screeched—the most awful sound: a cry of confusion and pain—and pulled into a tight little ball.

When the owl first came to the Home, Charlie had carefully wrapped bandages around Percy's broken wing. He'd mixed pablum and fed Percy with an eyedropper. He loved that owl. And he loved me, too. If we were dying in the desert, he'd give me his last sip of water. But sometimes I wonder who he'd think he was saving—me, or the weaker half of himself?

"Charlie?"

He turned and smiled as if I'd surely understand—after all, I cared for Percy, too. I must know what needed to be done to keep her close. I stepped inside the owl house. The moonlight faded as shadows crept over my shoulders. We drew together. Charlie's lips were white with bleach. Percy huddled inside her cage, peeping softly. Charlie's head doesn't even come up to my chin but I was the one who was shivering.

"I love you, Hen. Always have, always will."

"I love you, too, Char."

And really, I do. I *do*. He's all I have left of a family. Charlie's it.

My brother opened his arms to me. The pudding lid rested in my right hand. I'd cut my finger on one just like it months ago, nearly to the bone. Its edge held the moonlight falling through the roof: a curve of ghostly silver.

Now we're standing here, Charlie and me under the moon's cruel light. The first time we saw that moon, it was through the same eyes. Shadows tussle on the owl house walls, telling me that in this heartbeat or the next, something's bound to happen.

FRIDAY NIGHT
GOON SQUAD

The boy's fingernails. He'd bitten them down to the quick. He was only what, twelve? According to his file. *Oliver Gregory Lambert*. Resided at the Crestview Towers on Highland Avenue. The file didn't list his hair or eye colour but I could see those just fine: blond, green. His head was small, every feature squeezed tight, crowned by a blond mop. Cute kid. As a man? His head would have to catch up with the rest of him.

"You've been biting your nails, Oliver."

He shook his hands over his head as if he was pretending to be a chimpanzee. Then he sat on them.

"Nervous?"

"No, Missus Tolliver."

"Because that's why some people bite their fingernails."

We were in his mother's apartment. It was clean the way a boy's room would be if his mom had told him to tidy up before company arrived. If I were to open any of the closets, un-hung clothes would surely tumble out.

And I *could* open a closet: it was my job. Open closets and visit schools and look for bruises under shirt collars. It was my job to tick off boxes on a mental checklist, and if they toted up, I'd summon the Friday Night Goon Squad.

"You can get sick from biting your nails," I told him. "Your fingernails pick up germs, you see, then you transfer those germs to your mouth."

"I see," the boy said thoughtfully.

"Your mother never told you that?"

"Mom bites her nails, too."

His mother was outside. I'd asked to speak to her son alone and she'd agreed with good nature. She sat under a tree in the apartment's courtyard, smiling up at the sky. Her stomach was a swollen gourd.

"Are you excited about having a baby sister?"

Oliver sawed his forearm across his runny nose. His sleeve was crusty with mucous. *Tick.*

"A brother would be better."

"What's the matter with a sister?"

Oliver said, "Just a brother would be . . . tougher. You need to be tough."

"Girls can be plenty tough."

His mother was singing. *Hark! The voice of Jesus calling!* Her hair stuck out at hedgehog angles. She'd cut her hair herself—Oliver had told me she was scared of hairdressers. She didn't want anybody flying at her with scissors.

"Your mother's due soon. I'll be around more often."

Oliver's shoulders relaxed, and I was suddenly aware that he'd been carrying so much tension. "That's . . . awesome."

———

I returned to the Children's Aid Society to find a message from my ob-gyn's office reminding me of today's ultrasound. I scratched a note on Oliver's file—*obsessive nail biting?*—and headed out.

The waiting room was jammed. One pregnant girl paced with both palms pressed into the small of her back like a puppet dictator practising her coronation speech.

Paul showed up smoothing down his hair. His face had a lost, jumpy quality.

"Sorry I'm late," he said, folding his stork-like body into the seat beside me.

When my name was called I changed into a starched hospital johnny and sat on a padded bench in a dim room. The butcher paper crinkled under me. A graphic illustration of the female reproductive system hung on the wall. Fallopian tubes, ovaries, uterus, cervix, vagina. Yep, all present and accounted for.

The nurse smeared the ultrasound wand with Wavelength gel and slid it under the johnny. Frictionless cold spread across my belly—and behind it, the insistent pressure of the wand. She reached a free hand over my hip with the possessive, pushy way of nurses and shifted my weight towards her.

Goddamn it, be careful. You'll break something; you'll wreck it all . . .

An image flickered on the monitor. The amorphous body of an unshelled peanut topped with a bulbous head, resting in the hammock of my uterus.

The nurse called Paul in. The muscles bunched along the curve of my jaw. A bead of sweat trickled down Paul's face despite the coolness of the room. I suppose we may have looked more like witnesses to some incipient atrocity than expectant parents.

"The baby's turned around," the nurse said. "I can't get a look at the sex."

"Everything where it ought to be?" Paul asked in a casual, cocktail-party tone.

"As I said, I can't—"

"We don't care about the sex," I said. "Nothing's the matter?"

The nurse patted my hip as you might the flank of a nervy dray horse.

"From all I can see, you have a perfectly healthy child. You see that?" She pointed to the rhythmic dilation and contraction in the centre of the monitor. "That's the heart beating."

Our baby—*the* baby; *it*—was still so unformed, so *gelatinous*, that you could see its heart beating through its skin.

But it *was* healthy and that was . . . I quickly pulped that seed of hope. Stamped on it ruthlessly until it burst.

———

Some people shouldn't be parents. It's a bold statement, I grant you, but if you've worked this job as long as I have, it's one you'd get behind.

Five years. That's the shelf-life of your average child-services worker. You have five years before your worldview curdles. I was going on eight. I saw evil—real and verifiable *evil*—a lot of days. And it was banal: nothing elegant or Lecter-esque about it. Sometimes it possessed a certain rat-like cunning, but in general, the evil I confronted was rheumy-eyed and dull-witted and ignorant. Worst of all, that evil was filled with a sense of entitlement and unearned self-regard.

I hated some of my clients. This is an awful admission, but the world would be a better place without them. I hated the urbane schoolteacher who put a throw pillow over his daughter's face before slugging her. I hated the addict who left his jug of methadone-spiked OJ in the fridge for his five-year-old to drink, sending the kid into a somatic coma. I hated the patriarch and matriarch of a clan I privately called "the Stupids": I hated how the father would pound his fist on my desk, jutting the weak chin of his potato face at me while jabbering: "I'm trying to keep my family together, you bitch! That's my *job!*"

I tore up these unworkable family units, scattered them to the four winds, and I slept like a baby.

This morning, I had an appointment with Patrick Deakins. I wished he didn't exist, but he did. He showed up late, as usual. Patrick believed arriving late told me, and by extension *the system*, that he was not to be trifled with. He was a gargantuan, shaggy-haired sociopath.

He sat with a flourish, gathering up the folds of his cape and laying them primly across his lap. The purple velveteen gave off a whiff of deep-fryer fat.

"What is all this about, *Ms.* Tolliver?"

He drew out my name with a plummy, condescending flourish: *Miiizzzzz.* Beneath the cape, he was dressed all in black. Maybe he felt it was slimming, but there was no way to disguise his vein-shattering bulk. His turtleneck was stretched across the planetary plane of his gut so tightly that the fabric shimmered where the weave came apart, disclosing pinpricks of belly beneath. With his yellow corneas, jaundiced flesh and nicotine-stained fingers, Patrick looked like three hundred pounds of rancid butter stuffed in a dress sock.

"You're indicating you're *unaware* of why you've been called in, Mr. Deakins?"

I lifted my pen, set the nib on his file.

Patrick waved one hand in a manner that said I could set my pen down. "I know why *you think* I should be here."

"And why is that?"

Patrick's eyes peered at me from folds of flesh. They were framed by a head of messy curls—I could distinctly see a maple key in there—and a Brillo-pad beard that descended to his navel. I saw what I always saw in them: a veneer of feral intellect overlaying twin pools of festering rage.

"Don't you have that information in your little Filofax?" He spoke while peering down the slope of his nose at the file, trying to read what I'd written. I closed the folder . . . Then, realizing this was what he'd wanted, I opened it again.

"We have everything we need in here."

"Like what, pray tell? I have a right to know."

I stared at him evenly. "You really think so?"

"Don't I?"

"Tell me about the coffin, Mr. Deakins."

The last time I'd visited his home, I'd found a coffin in his living room, propped up on a catafalque. It fit in well with the matte-black walls and enamelled skulls and the stuffed raven.

"What about it?"

"Remind me what it's for."

"It's of religious significance."

"And what do you practice again?"

"Non-denominational neo-paganism. I thought you'd have that in your file."

"Did you purchase a lock for it?"

Patrick sniffed. "Why should I?"

"Because, Mr. Deakins, you have four-year-old twin daughters. Girls that age are naturally curious. We don't want them climbing into an open coffin."

We'd already taken the girls into custody once, a year ago, after I'd made an unannounced visit only to discover that Patrick had locked them in a closet so he could "get a minute's serenity." The wallpaper in the closet had been torn into thin strips—he'd left the girls inside so long that they'd *eaten* it in desperation. But thanks to our family-first protocols, the girls were back under his roof within months.

"It's a *coffin, Mizzzzz* Tolliver, not an abandoned fridge at the dump."

"The issue is not a matter of air supply. It's a matter of how inappropriate and quite terrifying it is for children to find themselves in a coffin."

"My daughters are not afraid of death. I've trained them not to fear."

Trained them. In that moment, I wished a scrap of plaque would detach from his arterial wall, float through his bloated body and flatline his heart. But I also knew that if I pushed too hard, this man might go home and shove his daughters into the coffin simply to prove he could.

"Get a lock as a good-faith gesture, then," I said. "The court looks favourably upon parents who accede to the token requests of their social worker."

"I own a crossbow," Patrick said breezily. "Several, in fact."

"And you're telling me this because . . . ?"

"Just an observation."

"No it's not, Mr. Deakins. I don't believe it is just an observation at all."

Patrick nibbled his wet bottom lip. The tip of his canine tooth was chipped.

"*Those* I lock up, *Mizzzz* Tolliver. Until I have use for them."

The phone rang. It was the principal at Oliver's school; he wanted me to come as soon as I could.

"I'll have to cut this short," I told Patrick, getting up.

"But I came all this way," he said, outraged, his little game interrupted. "I took the bus. At least reimburse me the fare."

Across the Horseshoe, in Niagara Falls, New York, you'll find a district called the Love Canal. Back in the '40s, the Hooker Chemical Company dumped 22,000 tons of toxic waste in a hole and covered it with four feet of clay. A few years later it was re-zoned for public housing for low-income families. The Hooker bigwigs made no attempt to disguise what was beneath the ground; they told the city: "Listen, under that clay is a reservoir of glowing green death." It was the city politicians who said: *Screw it—we'll tough it out.* Everybody *knew* what was lurking there, including the people who moved into those prefab units.

They were so happy to have a roof over their heads that they weren't troubled by what lay beneath their feet.

Random cancers in the area spiked, along with cases of infant epilepsy and deformations. Urinary tract infections skyrocketed. When the story hit the mainstream press, some people didn't get it. Why would anyone choose to spend their days perched atop a lake of disease?

But over on our side of the border—*we* got it. We understood how inertia could lock you into an orbit. A doomed orbit, sure, but an understandable one.

The route to Oliver's school took me down Portage Road where it snaked along the river. I could make out the Love Canal on the other side of the water, its tiered tenements obscured by the smoke pumping from the OxyChem smokestacks. The grey waters of the Niagara surged towards the head of the Falls; the pressure of all that tumbling grey—the equivalent of a million bathtubs a minute, according to our friendly tourist bureau— vibrated the car windows.

After the second miscarriage, our doctor said it might be the water supply. She'd said these words with her back turned, as though she couldn't quite bear to sign her name to the theory. Just something in the water.

Oliver sat on an orange cafeteria chair outside the principal's office, taking nervous bites out of an Eberhard eraser. He came to me arms-out and wrapped his hands round my waist.

"I didn't *do* anything," he said. "It was Mom."

I took his hand and went to see the principal, who looked like most principals I'd ever met: pot-bellied and bowlegged and wilted by the perpetual scorn foisted upon him by the student body.

"Oliver's mother came to school to see Mr. Wibbles," the principal told me.

"Who's that?"

"Mr. Wibbles is the class guinea pig," the principal said. "He is meant to teach the students about . . ."

"Responsibility," Oliver said. "We feed Mr. Wibbles and change his shavings."

The principal said, "This manner of things, yes. Oliver's mother is rather fond of Mr. Wibbles. This is the fourth time she's come to . . . play?" He glanced at Oliver, who lowered his head. "Yes, then, to play with Mr. Wibbles. Needless to say, a distraction."

I asked Oliver to wait outside. Once he'd shut the door, I said, "You've met Oliver's mother?"

"Briefly."

"So you recognize her shortcomings?"

The principal lowered one eyebrow. I went on.

"Oliver's mother scored 47 points on the Stanford-Binet Intelligence Scale. I imagine that's lower than most students here would score."

"I wasn't aware of that," the principal said. "She doesn't . . ."

"*Present*, is the word we'd use. Yes, at first blush she often doesn't *present* as having diminished capacities. But once you spend a little time around her . . . there is a childishness to Janet. She remains compelled by those things that only gripped us as children. Like guinea pigs."

"I'm sorry, but then shouldn't she ...?" The principal held his chin and peered at me with confusion, as though I were a math equation he was struggling to solve. "I mean, why is she the legal guardian of that boy?"

"Because she's Oliver's mother."

"Is it that simple?"

I nodded. "And because she loves Oliver and Oliver loves her. That's really the most important consideration. She's a good mother ... except when she's not."

"So ... you can take Oliver away?"

"Into care? Not unless I absolutely have to. Life for a child in care can be difficult. Sometimes the child feels hopeless. There is nothing unloving or hurtful about Oliver's home life. Janet is just ... absent-minded. But her errors have mainly been boundary-type ones, such as following her son to school so she can play with Mr. ...?"

"Wibbles. Apparently he wobbles, he nibbles, and so ..."

"Gotcha."

"In light of what you've said I'm bent by sympathy, but the situation being what it is ..."

"Say no more." I winked. "I'm on it."

Oliver was waiting outside the office, chewing on the second joint of his pointer finger.

"It's okay," I told him. "I'll sort things out."

"Good. I can't ... she can't just come into class and ..."

"*We* know that, right?" I waited for him to nod. "So now I just have to make sure your mom knows, too."

Doubt crept into his eyes. I set my hand on his shoulder.

"Back to class, Oliver."

Halfway down the hall he turned over his shoulder and said: "Tell Mom I love her still and all—okay?"

I found Oliver's mother in the library, sprawled on a beanbag chair. *Epically* pregnant.

"Hello, Janet."

"Hello, Missus Tolliver."

Janet was pretty in the way of a high school sophomore: there was an unfinished quality to her features, an illusory sense that they would change from what they were— plush but somehow blockish—into a truer, more adult kind of beauty. Janet had a body built for adult sex and a mind too much like a child's to realize the trouble it could get her into.

I pulled up a student-size chair and sat awkwardly, my chin nearly resting on my kneecaps.

"Janet, what are you doing here?"

She raked her teeth over her pillowy upper lip. "I know."

"You can't be coming here in the middle of the school day."

"I know, I know. I . . . got lonely."

"You don't see the other kids' moms here, right?"

"Right as rain."

Whenever I came to her home, Janet would try to give me something—a bag of peppermints or a music box that played "Alouette." *I can't accept those*, I'd tell her, and watch her face fall like a botched soufflé. But then her mind would fly elsewhere, and soon she'd be turning pirouettes across the kitchen floor.

She had one son and would soon have a daughter, each child with a different man, neither father in the picture. And she loved babies. She had told me so directly, eye-to-eye, with no hesitancy.

"Everyone loves babies," I'd told her. "Even ogres love babies. But babies grow up. They become boys like Oliver. Then surly teenagers, then men."

"I'll love Oliver when he's an old wrinkly man." Janet had giggled. "*Ogres.*"

I patted her knee and said: "Let's go someplace fun."

Janet said: "People are always promising fun, Ms. Tolliver. And then, I find out it's not really so fun."

"This will be. I guarantee."

I took Janet to the pet store. Paul and I had bought our beagle, Briar, there. It had been Paul's idea. And it was true what they say: the puppy required nearly the same attention as a newborn. When she whined in the night I'd put her in the bassinet beside our bed. Paul didn't like that, but at least the bassinet got some use.

"They have a rabbit," said Janet. "A *rabbit*, Ms. Tolliver."

The shop clerk opened the cage so Janet could pick it

up. The thing was *huge*—I wondered, morbidly, whether it had eaten its siblings. Rabbits did that sort of thing, didn't they? It seemed to be composed entirely of fur. A nightmare possibility entered my mind: that if you were to shave it, the rabbit would become increasingly smaller until you shaved it entirely out of existence and were left in a drift of fur . . .

"Aren't you beautiful," Janet cooed, cupping the rabbit by its bottom and raising it until their noses touched. "You're a very cute wabbit, yes you *aaare*."

The rabbit sneezed. Its whole body juddered.

"It's sick," Janet said, concerned. "Do you have a cough drop?"

"For the rabbit? No, Jan, that's not such a hot idea."

"Do you think I should take him home?"

I rubbed one of the rabbit's ears between my thumb and finger like a haberdasher assaying the weave of some exotic fabric.

"Your apartment's going to be plenty full." I let my finger trail down until it rested on the gentle swell of her belly. "Wouldn't you say?"

"Yep. That's about the size of it."

⸻

That night, I arrived home to a hallway cowled in smoky candlelight. Tea lights floated inside drinking glasses, illuminating the way into the kitchen.

Paul had made dinner. Quinoa and spinach salad and baked pork chops. He'd gotten the recipe out of our BabyFit book. He draped a tea towel over his forearm and presented me with a bottle of Perrier.

"Zis ees a subtle *eau* from France," he intoned. "Wiz topnotes of seltzer and a backnote of . . . uh, bubbles. Does it please madame?"

"It does."

Paul chased each bite with sips from a king can of Old Milwaukee. He was an artist by training, but his work had never earned much. He had misgivings about what he did; his blue-collar roots dictated that the only kind of paint under his nails ought to be whitewash. But I loved standing in his workroom surrounded by the beautiful things that leapt from his hands.

He was tall, and his body had a loose, windblown quality: it looked like it ought to be frightening crows in a farmer's field. But its appearance belied his strength and his capacity for quick violence. I'd seen his long arms lash like whips during a brawl at his high school reunion, when he'd got into it with one of the beer-gutted remnants from the football team's offensive line. Afterwards, he'd stood in the polar glow of the parking-lot light stanchion, absent-mindedly wiping his bloody knuckles on the hem of his dress shirt. I'd never been more purely aroused than I'd been in that instant.

"What are you thinking about, Pen?" he asked me now.

"Old times, is all."

The first one had died inside me. Its—*her*; we'd known that much . . . her insides wouldn't come into her body. I hadn't known before then that our organs develop outside of our bodies at first; they float in the amniotic sac, barely tethered to us, until some neat trick of biology pulls them inside where it's safe.

Our doctor had told us it was incredibly rare—the natal equivalent of Halley's Comet. *Incompatible with life*, was the term he'd used. Another doctor had removed her using a procedure called curettage. A very tiny vacuum cleaner inhales a very tiny thing. A little internal house-keeping. I tried not to listen as he did it—but how can you not *listen*?

Afterwards I'd only seen Paul's failings: how thin he was, consumptive even, his Adam's apple prominent as a baby's fist. His skin became translucent jelly in my eyes; I could see his tortured organs throbbing within that sapless frame.

But it wasn't as though he'd failed at his task, had he? The spark was there; it had even risen to a trembling flame. I was the one who couldn't hold onto it.

Paul came around the table. His long fingers crept up under my shirt, warm on the small swell of my stomach.

"Don't."

"Why not?" he said, all wretched innocence. "You can allow yourself to believe a little, Penny. Can't you?"

You can't. Not *ever*. The body can be deceitful. The body lies.

Hold on, I told myself, a desperate whisper I sent coursing through my marrow. *Hold on as tightly as you possibly can.*

———

A few weeks later, the phone rang in the still of night.

"Missus Tolliver? It's Oliver."

"Oliver? What time is it? I gave your mother this number for only the most serious emergencies."

"The baby's coming."

"Oliver, what . . . time is it?"

I glanced at the bedside clock. 3:13 a.m.

"There's water all over the kitchen floor." Fear snagged Oliver's voice and carried it to a register that would shatter glass. "And *blood*."

"Oliver, call 911 and tell them that your mother is having a baby. Can you do that?"

"Yes."

"Thattaboy. I know this is scary but it's okay. Hang up and call 911. I'll get in my car and—"

Click. Oliver had hung up on me. Smart kid.

By the time I arrived at the hospital, Janet was in the delivery room. Oliver was mooning around the waiting-room vending machine, idly pressing buttons—C4, L7— in the hope that something might drop from its coils.

"The ambulance driver was grumpy," he told me. He went back to punching buttons. The skin along the nape of his neck was inflamed. Had he been pulling his hair out?

I put a dollar in the coin slot and said, "Go wild." Oliver chose a roll of Certs.

"Seriously?" I said. "Of all the treats behind that glass, you go with Certs?"

Oliver stripped back the foil and thumbed one into his palm. "Nobody buys them," he said. "They sit there forever."

"Are you saying you feel sorry for the Certs?"

He offered me the roll. "They've got Retsyn."

We sat in the waiting room sucking Certs. Oliver told me the ambulance attendants had to snip his mom's underpants off because they were so bloody. They'd told Oliver not to look but he'd peeked through his fingers because his mom was crying so bad. He said he wished he hadn't peeked.

"I talked to the nurse," I told him. "Your mom'll be okay."

Oliver nodded. "Mom's tough. Mom's like . . . the silver ball in an old pinball machine, right? She just bounces around—*ping! ping! ping!*—and it's . . . nothing ever bothers her."

He bit down on his Cert. It splintered between his molars with a greenstick sound.

"What are you worried about, Olly?"

"Mom, she just . . ." Oliver's fingers gathered the denim over his knees, yanking and bunching until I could see the pale stems of his ankles. "She gets confused. She'll put a slice of bread in the toaster and forget that it's popped— she'll forget she was even *hungry*. But it's okay when it's just toast she's forgetting, y'know?"

After a while, I took Oliver's hand and together we walked down to the nursery. The newborns lay behind a viewing window inlaid with honeycombed mesh.

Oliver pressed his nose to the glass. "So tiny."

My fingertips found the glass. Unknowingly, of their own accord, they spider-crept up the window . . .

It happened very quickly, as it had before. An impossible circular tearing someplace inside, a crescent moon peeling free of the night sky. I sank to my knees—*no, no, nononono*—my hands clutching, pushing against the fall.

"Ms. Tolliver . . . ?"

"Get one of the nurses, Oliver. *Please.*"

═══

He was born while Janet was still in labour with her own child. He entered the world like a whisper. I barely felt him slip out.

He was twenty-five weeks. Nearly three months early. He looked like any other baby, except exponentially smaller. Those last three months are the growth stages, whereas the first trimesters establish the forms and functions, get the basics down. So that's what we ended up with: the beautiful basics.

He weighed less than three pounds. His face was a wrinkly walnut: his skull still needed to grow to make use of the extra skin. He was the most wondrous creature I'd ever seen.

When they opened his airway, he let loose a kittenish cry. The nurses wrapped him in a blanket and let me kiss and cuddle him. Then they took him away. My doctor came back looking grave. The prognosis for babies like ours was poor. They were cakes pulled from the oven too early: still soupy inside. He said this, although not those words.

The situation required that I look at things rationally, the doctor said. As if it was something I was capable of, if only I would set my mind to it. I told him I'd be keeping the baby. He dipped his chin and left.

Later, I overheard the nurses talking down the hall in the neonatal ICU.

"The poor thing's probably got a headful of mush," one of them said. "It'll rip the two of them apart."

"It usually does," said another one.

Paul accepted my decision. If I saw something struggling to express itself behind his eyes, I chose to ignore it. Everyone thinks it is so goddamn *easy*. You *fall pregnant*—the way you fall off a cliff. And for some, it really is that easy. It's the most commonplace miracle on earth—but still, a miracle.

Janet had her baby—a plump healthy girl—and toddled on home. I stayed with my own. Joshua. Once I'd made it clear I was keeping him, the hospital dutifully pushed the birth certificate through.

Joshua was kept in a clear plastic tub in the NICU. Twice a day I was allowed to hold him. I had to put on hypoaller-genic white gloves like a curator handling a priceless relic. His sunken eyes were netted in paper-fine wrinkles. His heart beat through every inch of his skin. I undid my shirt and slid him inside to feel his warmth against mine.

My phone rang. It was Oliver, breathing heavy.

"It's baby Hannah," he said.

I was at the hospital, visiting Joshua. Janet's file had been temporarily re-assigned. This was none of my concern.

"Calm down, Oliver. Talk slow. What happened?"

His voice dropped to a conspiratorial whisper. "Mom ran a bath for baby. Just half an inch of warm water, like the book said. But the phone rang and . . . when I went to use the toilet the baby was on her belly in the tub. She was . . ."

"Oliver, is she—?"

"I got her out. I sat on the toilet and lay her down with her stomach on my knees and rubbed her back. She coughed and spat water and then . . . she's breathing better now. But there are red worms in her eyes."

"Oliver, where is Hannah *now*?"

"In the bassinet in the TV room. Mom's watching *The Beachcombers*."

I hung up with wolves racing in my blood. I hit "4" on speed-dial.

"Officer Railsback? Angie? It's Penny Tolliver from the CAS."

"Evening, Pen. What foul wind blows you my way?"

"Saddle up the goon squad."

"Is it Friday yet?"

"Wednesday."

"Close enough."

It had begun as a morbid joke—sometimes those were the ones that got you through. "Child apprehension with officer assist," a.k.a.: the Friday Night Goon Squad. You hatch 'em, we snatch 'em.

I rendezvoused with Officer Railsback at the apartment complex. She must have felt the rage radiating off me.

"Everything okay, Pen? You need a minute?"

I made sure the car seat in my Toyota was firmly lashed down and said: "No time like the present."

It went fast. Railsback knocked on the door and I steamrolled in. Afterwards I couldn't recall much; it was like a waking dream. There was Janet sitting on the sofa, a placid look pasted on her face, grinning at me, arms open for a hug. I brushed past her and picked up the baby, noting the spots of blood in her eyes. Janet let out a sheep-like bleat when my intentions became clear. Oliver cowered in a

corner, shaking his head viciously. Janet began to scream—
"Don't you steal my baby!"—until Railsback had to restrain
her. The baby shrieked. My eyes narrowed and I hissed
something at Janet; I don't remember what I said but the
look I caught from Railsback told me I had crossed the line.

As I was buckling the baby in, Janet staggered onto
her balcony. "Give me back my baby! That *BITCH* down
there is stealing my baby!"

Other residents gathered on their landings, shouting
and cursing at me. Children's Aid did a lot of business in
Janet's complex. A bottle sailed out of the darkness and
exploded a few feet from my car.

"Everyone back inside!" Railsback hollered.

The residents retired. All except Janet, whose wails
took on the elliptical mourning quality of an air-raid siren.
Oliver crouched at her feet on the balcony with a hand
under each elbow, trying to hold his body together while
it shook itself to pieces.

Instead of driving directly to the office, I went to the river.

There was a spot I liked to visit, a place the tourists
don't know about. A narrow spit of land off the Dufferin
Islands, shoehorned out into the Niagara. The black water
surges around the huddled landmass, threatening to
submerge it but never quite doing so. In the summer, clover

grows over it in a thick tangle. At night, you can stand at its isthmus and see the pinprick lights of Goat Island.

I walked to the edge, two hundred yards from shore. Out here the river ran fast over a smooth dolostone bottom: the sound was like the tearing of silk sheets. The sky was suffused with stars; their distant light shivered with the rumble of the Falls. The baby, Hannah, was tucked safely in the crook of my arm. She slept: the rush of the water must've calmed her.

I remembered an experiment on spider monkeys I'd read about at work. Scientists took the baby monkeys away from their mothers at birth. The babies were given everything they needed—but everything came via inert mechanics. Their milk poured from a metal tube. They slept in moulds that mimicked the curves of their mothers' backs and stomachs, all wrapped in soft fur. Motherly sounds—coos and other vocalizations—were piped in over speakers.

The babies developed distressing tics. They tore out their hair and engaged in ritualistic self-abuse: slamming their skulls against the cage bars, biting their arms and legs. It drove them mad, to be separated from their mothers. I'd wondered why the hell the scientists would have required an experiment to tell them so.

Next, the scientists introduced sterile female monkeys to the babies. They latched onto one another instantly: the females adopted the babies as their own and the babies identified them as their mothers. More amazingly, some of the sterile females began to lactate. The babies socialized. The tics and self-abuse diminished. They became a loving social unit despite the fact that nature hadn't set them up that way.

I stood at the water's edge. My eyes travelled along the scrim of shore to the lights of Clifton Hill, to the Peace Bridge spanning the river, the grey ribbons of smoke unfurling from the smokestacks of the OxyChem plant and finally the squares of light burning in the Love Canal.

Poison. This whole place was poison, the ground and water and air. To stay was to let that poison leach into you. But to leave was to let go of everything you knew and the people you'd come to love—you'd all been poisoned together, a poisoned shot through to the soul, and the sickness was its own quarantine.

This was how you came to see the shape of your life in Cataract City. You were like a hardy plant growing in the thinnest crack: you expanded to fit the parameters of your enclosure, but grew no bigger. But a baby . . . when did the world begin to close in on a baby? Surely an infant couldn't see the walls of their enclosure. Surely it was, or should be, all open skies and endless horizons.

I stood between the water and the sky. The vastness of the possibility was dizzying.

When I returned to the hospital, Paul was bent over the tub that held our son, and when I came in he swivelled, smiling.

"The doctor says he's put on an ounce," he told me. "A whole *ounce*. Phenomenal, don't you think?"

Joshua did look fuller. He was fighting. That was a character of this place, too: fighting as a way of life. Paul's eyes fell to Janet's baby, who hung gently in her cradle at the end of my arm.

"Who's that, Pen?" he said softly.

"Work, darling," I said, just as softly. "It's only work."

MEDIUM TOUGH

The needle: 21 gauge, 1.5 inches. A hogsticker. I'd liberated it from the Thoracic Care unit; they stock cannulas for emergency chest decompression—you hammer one of those big-bore pins between the fifth intercostal to vent compacted air and blood. The contents of the syringe run as follows: 1 cc of Equipoise, a veterinary drug injected into cattle to render them fat and juicy, plus an additional 2 ccs of testosterone cypionate—i.e.: roughly twenty times the testosterone a man my size produces in a week. I've never been one for half measures.

Hormone replacement therapy? Already been tried. Creams, patches, gels, slow-release subdermal pellets sunk into my flanks. My hormones have flatlined, you see. Years ago, when he first examined me, my current doc gawped at my T-levels and said: "Sure you weren't born a woman, Jasper?" We're old pals; he can joke. Problem is, you've got to rub that goo on your hands to let the testosterone seep in—which is problematic, seeing as I handle loads of babies. Skin-to-skin transference, yeah? Good Dr. Railsback lays hands on little Janie Sue Macintosh, and next thing you know she's growing a beard.

I pump the stuff into my rear end. A fine pincushion. I can't use the hip because my sciatic nerve radiates from there; if the needle raked the nerve stem I'd be doing the noodle-legged cha-cha. And if I dumped the stuff directly into a vein it'd slam me into cardiac collapse. But fortune favours the brave, so tally ho! Into the ole keister.

I pierced the skin, aspirated, saw only the thinnest thread of blood and bottomed the plunger. *Yeeeeessss*—there's the heat-seeker.

I slipped the needle into a sharps bin and located the blister-pack of capsules. *Fludara*. An antimetastatic; it attacks the RNA, rots the helix and kills the spread. The label read: *Avoid inhaling the dust from a broken caplet*. The urge to crack one and snarfle it up my nose was awesomely powerful. I swallowed two, then two more. My tongue flirted absently around my mouth; the raspy white nodules on its surface raked my incisors, but they were too dense to burst. I heard my name on the PA.

Dr. Railsback to pediatrics . . .

The vulcanized orthotic spacer on my left shoe made a jazzy *dunka-dunka-dunk* on the hospital tiles. Up to the fifth floor. The air in the NICU was heavy with phero-mones. Aliphatic acids, which waft from the pores of women who've just delivered. A distinctive scent, with an undertone of caramelized sugar.

"Are we prepped?" I asked the nurse, Sandy, who herself smelled of cherry sanitizer. She nodded with remote calm—Sandy was the one you wanted intubating a preemie with a blocked airway.

"OR 5, Doctor Railsback. Doctor Beverly's finishing up with an epidural."

I prepped in a deep-basined metal sink. Shirtless—a quirk, but you really can't be too clean with surgery. One hand washed the other. The right: huge, thick-knuckled, bones lashed by a meshwork of heavy ligatures. The left: long and bony like the hand of Nosferatu. Metacarpals projected beneath the thinnest stretching of skin: the bones in a bat's wing. The right arm: a bowling pin-like forearm roped with freaky striations, a grapefruit-bulge of biceps. The left: a pair of sticks jointed at the elbow.

There's a line where the two halves of my body intersect. It begins to the left of my throat, centres itself between the points where my collarbones meet, cleaves the breastplate and ribcage then snakes to the left down my abdominals and carves right again before finishing at my groin. To the right: densely muscled, proportionate. To the left: austere devastation. The line of demarcation is plain: the vascular round of my right pectoral dips into a trough where it meets my breastbone and fails to rise again, exposing a flat expanse so devoid of muscle that every thump of my heart shivers the flesh. The ribs on my right are banded by stout tendons. The left ribs stick out like the spars of an unfinished boat.

My left side still *works*. The muscle, what there is, flexes. The nerve clusters fire. My left foot is 2.12 inches shorter than my right and my left arm 2.84 inches shorter than its mate—I had a colleague take the precise measurements. My face is unaffected. Should you see me walking down the street in trousers and long sleeves you would not, in passing, notice. Were we carnally acquainted, however, you might wonder if I'd not been born so much as *fused* from separate selves. During maiden intimacies it's my habit to disrobe slowly, explaining things. An educational striptease.

Dr. Beverly waited in the OR. Our patient lay on the surgical table, wracked with tremors—brainstem release phenomena. Isla, pronounced *Eye-la*. Beverly set her on the digital scale—3.55 pounds.

"I'll start on inhalants," he said. "Nitro to speed the uptake, then something with a slower wash-in. You looking for total bodily torpor?"

"I'll be inside her head, Bev. Can't have her squirming."

"Run with a quarter milligram of hydromorphone, but if she reverts to a pattern fetal circulation we'll risk acute hypoxemia."

Hypoxemia: CO_2 chewing black holes into Isla's brain. Beverly painted a mercurochrome square on her back and located the L3 caudal space between her spinal discs. The epidural catheter—a shiny segmented tapeworm—pierced the flesh in the square's centre. Isla's eyes, set in wrinkled webs of flesh, did not open.

Bev slipped a tiny mask over Isla's face, pumped in nitro to open her bloodpaths. He switched the drip to isoflurane, a powerful analgesic. Isla's chest shuddered. Infant breathing patterns can be random. You had to ignore them. The no. 12 scalpel rested in my left hand, classic pencil grip.

In med school the question had been: "Is Jasper Railsback surgeon material?" I wasn't the prototypical specimen, but I did possess the physical basics alongside the intangibles: force of will, self-confidence. Plus, there was the matter of my hands . . . true surgeons, or "blades" as we're known, are defined by our hands. Look at our fingers: willowy and tapered, seemingly possessed of an extra joint. A concert pianist's hands. A surgeon must possess extraordinary dexterity and be steady in the cut. You could eke by as an orthopaedic surgeon with so-so digits—that's basic, meatball surgery. But if you go blundering around in an infant's skull, tissue, organs, people die. In school we'd practised on bananas. Draw a dotted line on the skin, carve out the "lesion" using the slide cut technique. I'd bought bananas by the bushel—green specimens first, working my way up to speckly black ones. While my fellow students were exceeding the bursting-strength threshold and slicing into the banana "meat," my dynamite left was popping out perfect plugs.

My right is a bricklayer's hand. It can be taught blunt-force tasks. But I can feel music through my left hand. My right is my hammer. My left an instrument of God.

I began at the supraorbital node, five centimetres above Isla's nasal shelf. One must remember that an infant's bones are porous or in some cases nonexistent. Soft heads, flabby gizzards. The scalpel bisected the fontanel. I avoided the cortical veins running bluely under the skin and checked the incision before hitting the transverse sinuses. A brief freshet of blood. A lateral incision bisected the first: an X. I tweezed back the flesh, pinning the flaps down.

"Suction."

Sandy removed the occluding blood with a vacuum wand. Isla's brain shone within its encasement of cerebrospinal jelly. I searched for what I'd seen on the ultrasound: a tumour developing within the runnelled folds. A *teratoma*, as they're known: a congenital defect composed of foreign tissue such as muscle, hair or even teeth. Teratomas are rare; normally I'm looking for cortical dysplasia—a mutation of the brain cells—or pre-epileptic markers.

"That's a lot of blood," said Beverly.

"Coagulant, then, Bev."

He said: "Getting close to peak toxicity already, Jazz."

"Suction, Sandy."

I switched to the harmonic scalpel; it'd coagulate any severed vessels. Sandy slipped a pair of magnifying spectacles over my eyes; Isla's brain blew up in intimate detail. I spread the hemispheres with a pair of forceps; they pierced the cerebrospinal sac soundlessly. Oxygen licked at the pink loaves of brain, tinting the surface cells grey. I snipped nerve clusters, avoiding the corpus callosum, spreading the spheres farther until I could make out the vein of Galen.

There's an instant in any procedure when you understand that you hold everything in your hand. The God Moment. Each surgeon feels it differently. For me, this was a moment of awesome, near-paralyzing love. Love for the child beneath my blade: for its life and its capacity to do great things—or if not great, then merely valuable. And it was a moment of respect for their bodies, which I must invade, and for their futures, which I am dutybound to honour.

"Light, Sandy."

She illuminated the cranial vault. Below the hub of the angular gyrus sat a foreign mass: off-white and ribbed, crushed between the thalamic folds.

"I'm titrating up," Beverly said. "But I can't hold this level for long. She's nearing catatonic shock. Sandy, give me 4.5 ccs of plasma replacement."

She handed Beverly a syringe with a tablespoon of crystalloid plasma 3:1. I reached in with the forceps. The metal brushed Isla's olfactory bulb; her nostrils dilated involuntarily. I gripped the foreign mass, teasing it out.

"What in God's . . ." Sandy said.

A tiny, stunted foot. My forceps gripped its big toe. I grasped its neighbour and pulled gently. The toe released from the medullary fold with an audible *plik!* The entire foot came out slick with glia—brain glue, essentially. No calf, no knee. Just a disembodied foot, no bigger than a vitamin lozenge.

"Parasitic twin," I said. "Consumed in utero."

"Signs and wonders," said Beverly.

Two nights later I busted a poor guy's arm. Classic greenstick. Radius and ulna bones. I heard three percussive *pops!* as the flexor and brachii muscles unshackled from their moorings. Then the first of two wet, fibrous snaps: the ulna sounded like a pistol fired into wet sand. There's something mad about the sound of a bone breaking. It's a rip in the fabric of things, a glimpse into a realm of vast polar whiteness. Sounds silly, I know . . . after all, I break bones *purposefully* in the operating theatre, with a surgical chisel called an osteotome. With a controlled break, I'm in full command. But still: there is always that glimpse.

This particular break was not surgical, and it happened at the Ontario Arm Wrestling Association's Arm Melter event, the semifinals of which were held in the basement of the Knights of Columbus Hall on North Street. Low popcorn ceiling, steel cistern of gut-rot. A pair of padded arm-wrestling tables had been set up on the warped parquet. A passel of old Knights with suety faces slapped down dime-bets on the Crown and Anchor wheel. It was the type of crowd you'd expect when the roller derby passed through town.

I'd been arm-wrestling for years. Everyone needs a hobby and my credo is: Work to your strengths, baby! My right arm—*the gorilla*, I call it—is the perfect weapon. The battering ram to my left hand's lock-pick set.

My opponent was your standard Barbell Billy: fireplug-squat, vein-riven biceps jutting from a sheer wife-beater. He stuck his arm out as if he was *giving* me the damn thing. The ref cinched our hands with a leather thong to keep us gripped. When he said "Go!" the guy hit hard sideways, head down and snorting. Technique? Forget it! I fixed my elbow on the pad and let my shoulder absorb his thrusts. I felt the joint straining, and for a moment was mildly concerned that he'd pop my humerus knob out of its cup of bone and destroy that fragile arrangement, but it held and I was able to hook his wrist, get my knuckles pointed skyward and gradually peel his wrist back . . . which was when his forearm went kerflooey.

The bone-break shockwave juddered through my own body. My veins were so blitzed on adrenaline I kept trying to pin his wrist. In my defence, the guy wasn't aware of the trauma he'd sustained: the signals weren't routing through the proper synapses so his body kept fighting, that being the stubborn tendency of most bodies. Needles of dizzying white bled out of his limb from the points where the bone had shorn through. He stared at his assways-hanging arm, possessed of a surprising new bend, gave a quizzical half-laugh and said: "Huh." As if his arm were a riddle I'd solved.

There was something terribly intimate to that moment. Your instinct is to pull back, give the man space to bleed—but we were strapped together, right?

"I'm a doctor," I told my opponent, pointlessly.

He hiccupped in shock. I had him elevate the arm, our limbs still lashed together. I looked like a ref holding up a boxer's arm post-victory. Blood fell and freckled our cheeks. One of the Knights humped into the kitchen and came back with paper towels in one hand, a roll of aluminum foil in the other.

"This is all we got," he said to me. "We do Friday Fish Frys, not busted arms."

Afterwards everyone gathered outside in the cooling night. My opponent sat on the steps, arm mummified in bloody paper towels, waiting for his wife to show up.

"What the hell did you do to yourself?" she said.

We all laughed. That was how it was around this town. Do something idiotic and *male*, and you could expect your lady to give you both barrels.

The last light of day—briefly intensified as it slipped below the curve of the earth—jackknifed through the firs lining the road opposite us, a blade-edge of light limning the contours of my opponent's car, painting the side of his wife's face a mellow gold. I thought forward to the coming hours: that woman and her fella under the stark halogens of the ER, the bonesetter's tray, the crisp *snik!* as the carpals locked back into place, dissolvable sutures, coagulant and pain meds. Maybe she'd drive him home to their small clean house, and by then she'd have softened, forgiving him. She'd lead him into the bedroom as she might a child—he'd have a goofy oxycodone smile—settle him into bed, work her body against his with a look of concerned control. Hell, I'd suffer a broken arm for that. I'd suffer a dozen.

A Knight came over. Red fez cocked on his skull at a jaunty angle, face like a bowl of knuckles.

"One hell of an arm you've got, son. Too bad they aren't a matching pair."

His face shattered with laughter. You old prick, you.

——

"State your name for the record."

"Doctor Jasper Railsback."

"Place your right hand on the Bible and repeat after me: I swear to tell the truth, the whole truth . . ."

Welland Courthouse. Youth Services court. Three pew-like benches. Penny Tolliver, a Children's Aid Society worker, the lone spectator. One Crown attorney, one for the defense. The object of discussion: a ten-year-old boy with slight facial malformations. I sat in the witness box, having been summoned by the Crown.

"You operated on this boy shortly after he was born, Doctor Railsback—is that correct?"

"It is."

"Explain the nature of the operation—what did it address?"

"The boy's mother is a meth head."

"Objection," the defense council said. "Irrelevant."

The judge cocked her head at me. "Sustained."

"I operated on the boy, Randall, because his mother suffered a placental abruption. She suffered this because she smoked methamphetamine for the duration of her pregnancy."

"Objection. Conjectural."

"Sustained. Doctor Railsback ..."

I returned the judge's look evenly. "Due to the placental abruption, the boy was delivered early. He exhibited tremors, sleeplessness, and muscle spasms, which are symptoms consistent with infant narcotic withdrawal."

"*Objection*. Conjectural."

"Overruled. Could these be symptoms of other conditions, Doctor?"

"It's doubtlessly possible. Because of his early delivery, Randall's brain was not properly formed. He suffers from lissencephaly—*smooth brain*. His lacks the normal folds and grooves. The most common side effect is severely retarded motor skills. My procedure split the corpus callosum, severing the hemispheres in hopes of addressing those issues."

The Crown said: "Was it a success?"

"Most children with lissencephaly die before they turn two. If you're asking if the operation *cured* Randall, then no."

Crown: "Doctor, you mentioned his mother's substance abuse."

Defense, wearily: "Objection, your honour. What bearing?"

"I'll allow it."

"In your experience, Doctor, what are the—"

I said: "My mother was a juicehead."

Crown: "I'm sorry?"

"You must understand: A mother will never have more direct physical contact with her child than when she is pregnant. What she eats, the baby eats. What she drinks or smokes or inhales, so does the foetus. They share the same blood. The child's circulatory system is patched into hers. My mother was—*is*—an alcoholic. My father, too, though that has less bearing."

The defense rose. "Your honour, what bearing does *any* of this have on—?"

"Yes, Doctor Railsback," the judge said. "Where are you going with this?"

I rolled up one sleeve, then the other. Lay my bare arms on the witness box. The judge eyed them with interest. We're all rubberneckers, deep down.

"What people fail to grasp is how *sensitive* it is. A billion chemical reactions. A trillion tiny hurdles to be cleared. What happened to me was hormonal. A hormone is a key, you see; our cells are locked doors. If you've got the right key to fit the lock, the door opens. Well, one side of my body is all locked doors."

The judge said: "And this was a result of . . . ?"

"Of my mother pickling me in the womb. And listen, I've . . . *surmounted*. I'm a surgeon. A healer! But there's that line where love and basic concern butt up against weakness and addiction."

"Your honour, could we please—"

"This being a custody case," I said over the defense attorney, "my opinion on a personal *and* a professional level is that anyone who falls on the wrong side of that line ought to forfeit their child. Simple math."

Afterwards I stood on the courthouse steps in the ashy evening light. Penny Tolliver stepped out with Randall. The boy's facial features were consistent with his condition: the thin lips, temple indentations. His arm was wrapped around Penny's thigh, his head vibrating on the swell of her pregnant stomach.

"Thanks," she said simply.

"No prob, Pen. Part of the job."

I knelt before the boy. His left eye was foggy with cataracts.

"'You grow funny,'" I told him. "That's what a girl in elementary school once said to *me*. Greta Hillson with the golden curls. What a jerk, huh? But you know, she was right. I grew funny. But guess what, Randall? It's okay to grow a little funny."

Was that the literal truth? All I can say is that truth is twisty. The boy pressed his face into Penny's belly.

"Can I see you tonight?" she asked me.

"My door's always open."

———

I left Penny sleeping while I got up to medicate. My bare feet slipped across the hardwood to the window overlooking the city. The earthbound thunder of the Falls rumbled ceaselessly down the street-lit thoroughfares. Clifton Hill shone like a strip of tinsel. Tonight, at honeymoon haunts with names like Lover's Nest Lodge and Linked Hearts Inn, couples would bed down on scratchy motel sheets with the texture of spun glass. I liked the idea— that people I did not know, strangers I'd never meet, were happy and in love in the city of my birth.

To the south I could make out the oxidized metal roof of my old elementary school. In grade six, Ernie Torrens had busted my left arm. Yanked it between the bars of the bike rack, held me there as I squirmed. Took just one good kick. Ernie was a brutish creature with fingers constantly stained Popsicle-orange. Nowadays he's a grease monkey at the Mister Lube on Old Stone Road; he stands in the pit, eyes circled in grease-smeared flab, as my Volvo's chassis blots out his sun.

Back then, as I'd sat on crinkly butcher paper with a doctor setting my arm bones, I knew I'd have to act. Lie down too many times—make a habit of showing your soft belly—and you'd forfeit the spine it took to get up. I brought a tube of airplane glue to school and ran a thick bead around the toilet seat where I knew Ernie always copped a squat before recess. His confused bellowings were auditory honey to me. He tore skin off his backside trying to stand. The firefighters were called but before they arrived the janitor attempted to loosen the bond with some manner of chemical solvent; it reacted with the glue, scalloping Ernie's thighs with a first-degree heat rash. The firemen unscrewed the seat from the bowl and led him out to the truck. Ernie didn't even get a chance to wipe.

Later, we were both summoned to the principal's office. I leaned towards Ernie and whispered: "You're strong but I'm smart. I'll hurt you worse."

Ernie laid off after that, but others didn't. My childhood was a procession of bowl-cut, feebleminded tormentors who all earned harsh, quixotic reprisals. Eventually the message spread among our city's bully population: *Don't bother with Jasper. Seek easier meat.* But it was a message writ in blood, as much mine as theirs. The hospital's staff psychologist had once asked, during my mandatory annual appointment, if the years of bullying had compelled me to make one side of myself as powerful as possible.

"Look at Ziggy Freud over here," I'd said. "You've pinned my id to the wall."

I turned from the window and headed into the kitchen. I always medicated on the polished granite of the butcher block—I kept it sanitary, like the OR. My pills were in the fruit bowl. I popped four Nolvadex, an anti-estrogen med, two Proviron, two Fludara.

I cracked the fridge, found the pre-mix of HCG behind the cocktail olives. I was unwrapping an insulin needle when Penny came in. The harvest moon fell through the east-facing window to gloss the swell of her stomach.

"What's that?"

I said, "Truth serum."

"Oh?" she said. "You'll tell me all your secrets?"

"It's human chorionic gonadtropin," I said. "Testosterone regulator."

"I love when you talk shop, Jazz."

"It's derived from the urine of pregnant women, don't you know. I take 250 IUs weekly, spread out in 50-IU doses. The synthetic testosterone I inject converts into estrogen. *Aromatizes* is the word."

"I like the sound of that. Aromatize."

"Gotta take my meds so I don't get gynecomastia. Buildup of breast tissue, yeah? Otherwise I'd develop a lush set of man-cans. Except I'd only get one, on my right side."

Penny cupped her own breasts. "Mine are huge."

"They'll get bigger. Wait until your milk drops."

She took the needle. "Where do you want it?"

"Deltoid. Medial head."

She swabbed my shoulder with rubbing alcohol, jabbed the needle.

"It could be yours, Jazz."

"Pen, please."

"What?"

"You know who you're fucking, don't you? I'm a eunuch, Pen. I've been playing silly buggers with my body chemistry and I still produce barely enough testosterone to put hair on my nuts. Plus I was tested. I told you that."

"You say so, but—"

"My swimmers are not viable, Pen. Mutation levels sky-high. Two-headed swimmers. Or no heads at all."

Put my seed under an electron microscope and you'd see platoon upon platoon of headless, legless, useless soldiers. Sometimes an image hit me, unbidden, at the instant of release: a flood of broken-limbed bodies and horribly mutated forms sheeting over an austere landscape. Unmuscled arms and sightless eyes and corkscrewed appendages divorced from their husbanding bodies—no connectivity, no purity of form. A tidal stew of sexless, mismatched parts.

But if I've somehow been robbed, karmically speaking—well, then, it's only in relation to normal people, the average life possibilities. And I've never been normal. Not for one moment of my life. Since birth, every second of my existence has been borrowed against fate. But we're all on an extinction clock; the hands just circle a little faster on mine.

"It only takes one," Penny said. "You'd make a good dad." Her fingers traced her belly. Her bellybutton had popped out. "Anyway, I could lose it."

"Don't talk that way, Pen."

I'd met Penny when she'd lost her first child. Then again later, when the second one passed. A third survived a few days. It had gastroschisis: born with its organs outside its body. I never got a chance to operate. It would've taken an act of God, anyway.

"You'd make a good dad," she said again.

I plucked an orange from the fruit bowl and squeezed convulsively. The rind ruptured, spilling juice down my forearm. This was a trick I pulled out at parties; I'd get drunk, pulp a whole sack of them. The Juicer.

"You know who else'd make a good dad, Pen? Your husband."

"Cruel."

Why dispute it?

⸻

The Arm Wars Classic finals took place in the parking lot of the Americana Motor Lodge, a hop-skip from the flesh pits at the ass-end of Lundy's Lane. The night was humid. I felt the high-hat beat of my heart where my throat met my jaw.

I'd been training on a jury-rigged pulley system in my garage: One end of the cable was attached to a U-handle, the other to a milk crate. I loaded the crate with weight plates, gripped the handle and pinned it down. I'd worked out after my skeleton shifts at the NICU, inching my way up to nearly three hundred pounds, quitting when my wrist began to make pop-grind noises.

I bought a Labatt Blue from an old Mexican gent selling them out of an orange picnic cooler and scanned the contestants. Many were wearing yellow T-shirts that read *I'M PULLING FOR YOU.* I milled with the crowd, relishing the tightening inside my chest: a thousand disparate threads pulled from each muscle group, pinching themselves towards a centre of singular purpose.

My opponent was a cask-bellied brute in a John Deere cap. He set his elbow on the pad, tendons protruding from his neck. I smiled slightly. It didn't matter if a guy had sweeping back muscles or a striated chest; arm wrestling required a specific kind of strength, concentrated in the wrist and fingers, the biceps and shoulders. I had that. And beyond that, I had the grinding, golem-like power to demoralize my opponents.

I dusted my hands with chalk. We locked up. The guy grooved deep into the webbing between my thumb and fingers, trying to preemptively break the plane of my arm—if he could peel back the wrist and come over the top, the match was won.

I disengaged, shaking my arm out. The adrenaline was jacked into me now—that familiar ozone tang at the back of my throat. We locked up again. The grip was pure. Spectators clustered round. The ref straightened our wrists.

"Go!"

My opponent pulled hard, sunk in the hook, dropped his thumb and came over in a smooth, quick move. My arm bent back. The cartilage in my shoulders shrieked. My hand was two inches from the pad but I held it. The big bastard torqued his shoulder, bearing down, screaming: "*Reeeeagh!*"

I hissed air between my teeth, popped my opponent's thumb and broke the hook. My biceps were spiderwebbed with veins, flushed pink with pressure. I jerked my arm in a series of hard upward pops, each one budging the guy's arm. I shifted instinctively, slipping my thumb over my opponent's first knuckle and finding my own hook, bearing down with ceaseless pressure. This was my element: the slow and steady grind. The big man's wrist folded back, steel gone out of it. His shoulder gave out next. His whole body went from a power posture to a crumbling one. I worked steadily, inching him down . . .

Suddenly, a wave of teeth-splitting coldness rolled through me. Something awful was happening inside my chest: it felt as if each organ there was unlocking itself from the stronghold of my body.

The big guy folded his wrist back over and cranked my arm back.

"Winner," the ref said, holding up the big man's hand.

I wiped spittle off my chin. "Good pull," I congratulated him.

Ten seconds later I was humping across the road, squinting against the glare of onrushing headlights, and over the crushed gravel of the breakdown lane to the Sundowner. I tipped the tuxedoed bouncer and settled into a seat on pervert's row.

The girl on stage had rudely-chopped dark hair and lean, articulate limbs that seemed to swivel on servos. She channelled an android's aura: a futuristic pleasure model, all ballistic rubber, frictionless nylon and silicon grease. As she rode the brass pole, her expression was one part massive boredom mingled with two parts existential despair. When the song ended she stepped off the stage and took the chair next to mine. Her hand fell upon the baguette of flesh and bone that was my left thigh.

"Buy a gal a drink?"

The waitress took my twenty and returned with a glass of water for the girl.

"Pricey *agua*," I said.

"It's from a glacier."

"I don't normally come to places like this," I said, unnecessarily.

"Nobody ever does, man."

She asked if I'd like to have sex. I said yes without giving it much thought. She disappeared behind the stage's tinsel curtain and came back in a tracksuit.

The night sky was freckled with clear, cold stars. We walked to the Double Diamond motel, past its leaf-strewn swimming pool hemmed by waist-high chainlink. Her room was small and neat and smelled of carpet freshener. She threw herself on the bed in a childlike way: her butt hit the mattress, bouncing her up. She sloughed her sweat-shirt off in a manner some might've found charmingly unpretentious, but to me seemed sloppy and careless.

"Three hundred bucks," she said.

"Okay. What do we do now?"

"Need a refresher on the birds and bees? You can tell me what to do, if you'd like."

"Just give me the usual."

"Ah. A traditionalist."

She gripped my hips. Unbuttoned my pants, slid them down.

"Your legs ..."

She seemed fascinated rather than horrified—either that, or she was the consummate pro's pro. I slid my shirt up to show her my stomach.

"You're like that all the way up?"

"To my neck, yes."

She fished her hand through the fly of my boxers. Her touch was dry but gentle. "Feels like the standard apparatus."

A fragile voice said: "Mom ..."

The boy had stepped through a door that connected to the adjacent room. On first glance I understood he'd been dealt a common genetic indignity. His chest had a telltale shrunken look. The girl snatched her top, slid it on, and went to him. I pulled my trousers up.

"What's wrong?" she asked the boy, who was perhaps six.

"Thirsty."

The girl gave me a tight smile and held up one finger—*give me a minute.*

"Take your time," I said. "In fact, I could use some water myself."

I walked into the next room, which clearly they shared. There were open suitcases, the smell of cough syrup and body butter. In the bathroom I unpacked two motel glasses from their paper wraps. I smiled at my reflection. Blood climbed the chinks of my teeth. I swished water around my mouth, spat it red-tinged down the drain.

The boy rubbed sleep crust out of his eyes and accepted the glass I held out. He drank, coughed a little, breathed heavily.

"CF?" I asked his mother.

"How can you tell?"

"I'm a children's physician."

Cystic fibrosis. Gene mutation. Hallmark symptoms: poor growth, low muscle tone, high incidence of infertility. The boy and I were practically brothers under the skin.

"Show him," she said to me.

I sipped water, regarding her over the glass's rim.

"Please."

I peeled my shirt off, flexed my right bicep. A single ticket to the gun show.

The boy said: "Are you sick?"

"Aaron," his mother said. "That's not nice to ask."

"Yes. I'm sick."

"You're not going to die, are you?"

"*Aaron*."

"Not right here in front of you. I'll hold on a bit longer, I promise. Do you know where I was tonight, Aaron? An arm-wrestling contest."

The boy said: "Did you win?"

"Not this time, but I've won before. Here, I'll show you how."

I had him sit on one side of the room's small table while I sat on the other.

"Lay your arm on the table for me."

Obediently, he did so.

"Let's work on your form, Aaron. Your butt's stuck way out for starters; scoot up, get closer. Now your arm's too straight; bend your elbow, get your hand closer to your chin." I gripped his hand. The bones were birdlike. "Now you've got all the leverage and I've got none. Technique is what evens the odds. Doesn't matter how strong or fast your opponent is if you've got him beat on technique."

I wanted to tell him: *Life is* all *technique. The world is full of us, Aaron. The mildly broken, the factory recalls and misfit toys. And we must work a lot harder. Out-hustle, out-think . . . out-technique.*

"Now if your opponent cranks your arm, don't panic. You can rest with your hand nearly pinned—the shoulder joint will prop you up." I pushed his arm back gently, demonstrating. "Feels stable, doesn't it?"

"Yeah."

"Let your opponent exhaust himself, right? Then it's your turn. Concentrate on turning your hand over, pointing your knuckles at the sky. Try it, okay?"

The boy turned his hand over, peeling my wrist back.

"See? Now *you're* in control. And your opponent wants to quit. So *make* him."

The boy bent my arm back. "You let me win," he said.

"I did. But I'm an adult and I've been doing this a long time."

His mother tucked him back into bed. She cocked her head at the neighbouring room and said, "Still want to . . . ?"

"It's okay."

I reached for my wallet, but she trapped my hand inside my pocket. We stood in the gauzy half-light. My cellphone chimed. Code Blue at the hospital.

I hotfooted it back to the strip club and got into one of the queued taxis. As it wended down Lundy's Lane through pools of streetlit incandescence, I dialed the NICU and got Sandy on the line.

"Premature birth," she said. "Signs of IVH."

Intraventricular hemorrhage. Excessive pressure on the preemie's skull, causing blood vessels to burst.

The cab dropped me off at the ER. I shouldered through the swinging doors, moving fast, adrenaline—the only hormone I produce in adult-human allotments—blitzing through me in a powerful wave.

I stripped off my shirt in the prep area, lathered with carbolic soap and exfoliated the topmost layer of bacterial cells. A short hallway connected the prep area to the main surgical suite. The route took me past a series of glass-fronted OR rooms. In the final room, I saw Penny. I got only a flash—the blood, Penny's husband gripping her hand—before stepping into the surgical suite.

Penny's baby lay on the operating table. It—*he*, a boy—was covered in cottage-cheese-like vernix; his cheeks were feathered with lanugo hair. Dr. Beverly had strapped a mask over his mouth and nose.

"I've got him on a low dose of desflurane," Beverly said. "There's not a lot of brain activity."

I thought, but did not say, the buildup of blood may have been screwing with the neurological rhythms. I selected the thinnest cannula needle: the gauge just wide enough to let the platelets out single-file. The procedure was tricky: pierce the fontanel and thread between the hemispheres into the ventricle shafts. Release the blood and bleed off the pressure without forfeiting too much cerebrospinal fluid—otherwise the unprotected brain would bounce against the skull case and the exterior layers might slough away, killing motor function and the acute senses. It would be purely a "feel" operation—the equivalent of searching for water with a witching wand.

I positioned the needle in the centre of the fontanel "diamond," the four corners where the skull bone had yet to join. The tip dimpled the skin and slid in without resistance. I crouched, training my gaze tightly. It always amazed me just how wonderful newborn babies smelled. The world had yet to lay its marks on them.

"He's spasming, Bev," I said. "You've got to stabilize."

The rubber hose feeding into the mask was kinked. Gingerly, Beverly removed the baby's mask . . .

"Doctor Railsback?" It was Sandy's voice: distant, tinny. "You okay?"

The slope of this child's nose . . . The fingers of my left hand tightened ever so slightly around the needle's shaft. My fast-twitch fibres vibrated like overtuned piano wires. *It only takes one.* Jesus. Signs and wonders.

"Jazz, pressure's building."

I unscrewed the stent-clamp. A pressurized stream of blood jetted out. I willed myself to calm down—*begged* my body to do as it was told.

"Pressure's climbing," Beverly said. "We're getting erratic spikes on the EEG."

I pulled the needle back a half inch, adjusted the angle and reinserted. I'd be flirting with the pituitary gland.

We are all children of eggs. An Ashanti proverb I'd read a long time ago. And yes, it is true: we start that way. We are all flawless at conception. But consider the ways things can go wrong: a defect within the zygotic membrane, an erroneous replication in the DNA chain, a chromosomal hitch, a slight mis-expression of a critical peptide . . . imperfections so tiny that the strongest electron magnification provides but a shadow. They are unmeasurable in the truest sense, so too often we measure them the wrong way. They take on the weight of fate. The progenitor's sins passed down the bloodline. Such flaws are pearl-like: a body shapes itself around that tiny speck of grit. The pure mathematics of a healthy, functioning body and mind are staggering.

"We're black-spotting," Bev said. "We're going dark in there . . ."

I gave the cannula the gentlest half-twist, hunting for the pocket. The steel slipped effortlessly through the folds, through storms of neutrons snapping between those awakening synapses . . .

You've got to be tough for contingency's sake. My mother had been tanked to the gills when she'd told me this. She'd left a stove element on, and I had touched it. My right hand still bears the concentric scar. She had cavalierly pressed ice to the burn, never setting down the jelly jar of vodka-lime in her free hand. *You're only medium tough, kiddo,* she'd told me. *Right in that meaty part of the curve.*

There was weakness inside me. Some nights I felt it as a discrete entity: constantly shifting and ungrippable, nothing I could seek out or eradicate. As much part of me as my organs and flesh, inseparable from whatever goodness of character or strength of will I might otherwise possess. And my witching-hour fear is that this inborn weakness—marrow-borne and incurable—will find its deepest groove inside me at the worst possible instant.

And so I bloodhounded that phantom pressure, grappling with rising terror that found its outlet through my fingertips—be *still*, for God's sake, please. The needle's tip inching through the dark inside the boy's skull as one pure, clean thought blitzed through my own furied brainpan: *O my son my boy my son my baby baby boy.*

FIREBUGS

There are shapes that only live in fire.

Hunger. That is fire's basic drive. It is the purest, most incarnate hunger you can imagine. I've seen fire chew through lead girders: they soften and bend over backwards like contortionists. I once saw a column of flame ripple up a sheet of aluminum siding so that it crinkled and contracted— the sound of ice cubes fracturing in a glass—and curled right up as if rolled by huge, invisible hands.

Fire will grunt and growl and come at you with the soft slithering of a snake. It'll howl around blind corners like a pack of wolves, and gibber up from flame-eaten floorboards and reverberate in a million other strange ways besides. Sometimes it sounds like buzzard talons clawing across pebbled glass. Other times, it'll come for you silent as a ghost: a soft whisper of smoke curling back under a doorway, beckoning you to open it. That's when it's most dangerous—when it's hiding its true face.

One thing people don't get is that there's a sturdiness, a solidity to fire, which may seem odd, seeing as it's flexible, too, happy to shape itself around its host. But I've seen it punch holes in walls and carry roofs off houses. I've watched a rope of flame rip through a backyard elm quicker than a chainsaw.

But its most lethal quality is its ability to take on shapes. Fire holds the most nimble, the most uncanny and breathtaking shapes. It strolls and eddies and curls like tidal breakers. A person can stare into the shifting centre of a fire and see . . . well, everyone sees something different.

The shapes you see in fire echo those with which you are familiar, those you understand. You believe you're watching creatures of smoke and char breathing themselves into existence. The shapes become more beguiling the closer you get to the flashpoint—when the heat will steam the marrow in your bones.

Jerry Ullness, good friend of mine, a twenty-year vet on Ladder 11—I saw him fall into a fire. He dropped his axe and raised his palms like a penitent evangelical welcoming the Lord into his heart.

It happened on a narrow staircase inside a firetrap off Morrison Street. The blaze had taken root in the basement and twined through the walls like ivy, crawling up the electrical wires with orange fingers. The flames licked up under the stairs and gnawed through the wood; the stairway toppled into a roaring pile of cinders directly in front of poor Jerry. For a second, he teetered on the precipice, peering down into drifts of glowing coals. I know he saw something. What, I couldn't say.

"No, Jerr . . ." I breathed.

But he was gone. Bewitched by the shapes. They were like the sirens in the old myths, calling from the jagged rocks to lure sailors to their doom. You get caught up in the shapes of fire, give yourself over to them, and by the time the flames reach out, you'll go willingly enough.

I told Jerry's wife it was smoke inhalation, said he'd passed out. It was the simplest explanation. Hell, maybe it even happened like that. She had him cremated. Truth be told, Jerry was pretty much there already.

Part of me was jealous. A small part, but . . . I wanted to see what he'd seen.

———

I was born Blake Kennedy Jr., on a hazy July evening at Cataract City General. A serial arsonist was at work that summer, and the city was burning. My mother said I was born with old fires racing through my blood.

That summer's pyromaniac was a cagey bastard with a flair for the theatrical. He'd bust into a vacant home, crack open the Bakelite casing of the rotary phone, attach a wire to the ringer, and thread it down to a jug of gasoline. Then he'd hightail it to a bank of pay phones and plug a dime in the slot and place a call. The spark of the ringer travelled down the wire to set the gas aflame.

The local rag hired a headline writer with a tabloid background.

Dialing for Disaster! Calling for Conflagration!

When a head-shrinker postulated that the guy might've been setting fires to satisfy odd lusts, the headlines ran salacious: *Pervy Pyro's Phallic Phone Party!* And *Freaky Firebug a Blaze-Setting Bedwetter!*

They never did catch the guy. A few of the fire-gutted houses stayed that way for years; as a kid, I remember those whistling black skeletons dotting the city grid, charred plots where the sunlight went to die. Fire can reshape any city— take away its profile, reduce and flatten it. The ultimate eraser.

Growing up, I was a bit of a firebug myself. I'd light paper caps with a magnifying glass. Make a homemade flamethrower by holding a lighter up to a spray can of Pledge. Lord! Small wonder a lick of flame didn't travel back up the nozzle, ignite the pressurized contents, and blow my face off. But I don't suppose I'm the first guy to have used up eight of his nine lives in boyhood.

Turns out I wasn't even the biggest firebug in our family. But we'll get to that part of the story later.

That I'd become a firefighter wasn't exactly shocking; a lot of us were fire-setters as children. The polarity shifts: you want to stop fires rather than start them—but fire-fighters end up setting a lot of fires anyway, under the auspices of knowing thine enemy. You learn its tricks and tendencies in order to conquer it.

Which is a mistaken belief. You can't conquer fire any more than you can any classical element. Such forces are immortal and unfeeling. All you can hope is to divert them from humanity.

I became a firefighter—a "jake," as we call each other—right out of college, and held that job for fifteen years. Then I snapped an ankle fighting an air-fed flashover in the Hot Box, a three-storey metal latticework where we staged controlled blazes. It healed badly. I couldn't meet the baseline physical competencies. Chief said, Sorry, Blake, but you've got to hand over your axe.

So I don't fight fires anymore. I investigate them. I belong to the aftermath now, sifting the ashes for the hows and whens. The whys you may never know—and that's something else you've got to make peace with.

Lately I've been busy. The city's burning again.

=====

Detta Wilson. That's the name of the latest victim. "Odetta" is the name on her birth certificate, but she was Detta to her friends. Seventy-four years old. Cashiered for forty years at the drugstore on Drummond. Was a devoted parishioner at St. Paul's Evangelical. Widowed with two loving adult children. Black, but race didn't appear to come into it. Having a busted smoke detector and being a sound sleeper did come into it.

The incendiary rig was a plastic milk jug full of gasoline with a homemade wick. It's a simplistic device: you just light the sucker and leave it on someone's front stoop and walk away. It's not going to go up right away. Gasoline, the liquid, that doesn't burn. It's the gas vapours that are flammable. The jug burns at a slow smoulder until the flame dips inside the mouth, melts the plastic, and lets the fuel escape.

The gas would have caught with a soft *whuumph*, like the wind bellying a boat sail. Next, the fire would have chewed the latticework to where Detta lay slumbering.

It pissed me off—all of it, but the method pissed me off the worst. A gallon of gas in a milk jug with an old rag for a wick. By the time it did its damage, our boy would've calmed his wild eyes and sweated off the greasy stink of gasoline. Two bucks' worth of material and a seventh-grader's grasp of science. Poof—a good person gone to vapour.

Our boy was nothing but a dog who'd learned a very simple trick. But it was a trick he'd performed eleven times in the past six months, by my count.

"We've got to ferret this firebug out," the chief inspector told us. "Every bug's got a routine. Suss out this nut's."

The problem was, our boy didn't hold to any pattern in his targets. Tenement row houses, brownstones, duplexes. Single-family dwellings, apartment foyers, warehouses that lay uninhabited but for the rats. Men and women, geriatrics and kids, black and white and red and yellow.

I stuck push-pins into a map of the city for each site he'd torched: hopelessly random. He operated by no known logic—not even the herky-jerky logic of a pyro. All I could say for certain was that our boy seemed satisfied to see things go up in smoke.

I returned to Detta's house the day after it burned. She'd made it out alive but succumbed to smoke inhalation a few hours later. It was mid-afternoon, and wedges of terra-cotta sunlight burned between gaps in the city skyline.

The fire continued to die inside the house, with a thousand sly cracklings and crimpings as the heat seeped from scarred metal and wood. The east- and south-facing walls of Detta's home had burnt to the studs. The brickwork had checked its progress in the other directions, so the fire had done what fire always does: it wormed between the floors, feeding on the dust and hair and seventy-odd years' worth of dead skin trapped under the boards; my old instructor had told us that a human being sheds nine pounds of skin per year.

Old man's beard? he'd said. *Yellowed newspapers? Dry human skin has those beat all to hell. Skin's the ultimate tinder.*

What remained was a near-perfect cross-section of the interior, the kitchen and bathroom and master bedroom laid out, their contents smoke-damaged but intact. Detta's claw-foot tub tilted at an impossible angle from the charred second-storey floorboards. A nightgown fluttered on a hook near the bedroom window, which firefighters had smashed to let the smoke escape. It reminded me of the Barbie Dream House my sister had as a kid, the one that split open down the middle to present its guts.

I grabbed my kit and ducked under the yellow police tape. The fire had trickled off the porch to ignite the dry lawn. The branches of a mulberry bush hung in blackened spears, the ribs of a denuded umbrella.

The porch was ash. I braced my palms on the foundation and powered myself up to where the doorway once stood. The structure had been hosed down—water dripped off the scorched cornices and the obsidian-dark points of shattered glass—but I could feel the latent heat trapped in the brick.

Investigate enough arson cases, and you'll understand just how reductive fire can be. It robs all things, be they natural or forged by human hand, of colour and texture. Objects either become light as ash or attain a shocking heaviness. Once, after a restaurant blaze, I'd found a stack of skillets smelted into a solid mass, so heavy I couldn't lift it. A vulcanized sheen drapes everything, as if it has been dipped in a pool of rubber at a tire factory. That breed of blackness hurts your eyes.

I stepped over the floorboards to the wooden banister, now a row of black spikes. The carpeting on the stairs had fused to the underlying wood. The billowing circular smoke pattern on the walls indicated that the fire had carried itself swiftly up the staircase before the low ceiling had checked its progress, creating a dead zone of air circulation and denying it the oxygen it needed to thrive.

I calculated that Detta had two means of escape: the upper-storey windows or the stairs. She hadn't jumped. But the staircase would have been consumed in flames by the time she'd woken up . . .

I flipped open the kit and grabbed a few surgical pads. I blotted the ash-thickened water on the stairs, sprinkled the staircase with flash powder and let it settle. Then I switched on the hydrocarbon detector.

People believe a fire erases all signs of evidence. Not so. Sure, plenty of clues get incinerated—witnesses, too, sadly—but we inspectors have our ways. The hydrocarbon detector displays trace amounts of carbonized natural matter on any surface. In most cases, that means human skin.

The detector picked up footprints, one on each stair. Detta had run down the staircase while it was on fire. I imagined her rushing down the stairs, taking them one at a time, trying to tiptoe, maybe, the flames curling under her flannel gown, licking between her lips to blister her lungs . . .

Twelve stairs. Twelve footprints. Twelve swaths of flesh in the exact shape of feet, like boot-prints in the snow, each one incrementally smaller than the last.

Detta's skin would have fused to the stairs instantly—these are known as thermal fusion burns, where the trauma occurs deep in the subcutaneous tissues—and she'd have torn away her burnt flesh as she progressed. That raw skin would have hit the second stair, fused, torn free again. Her feet would have become smaller and smaller, the way a

Russian doll shrinks as you unpack it. Had the staircase been long enough, I suppose Detta would have run her feet clean off.

Did our boy know what hell he was wreaking? He worshipped at the altar of Vulcan, and his god was a violent one. Vulcan liked nothing so dearly as to ignite the world in flames and stand by as it burned.

The next day, I drove to the facility on Wellington Street. My baby sis, Franny, was a permanent resident there.

My sister is the sweetest, most trusting and gentle soul—but there's something not-quite-right with her mind. She's soft in the attic, people around here would say. What I think is that some people aren't built for the daily rigours of life, is all. Franny has always had this innate connection to the weak and the innocent, to the birds in the sky and the beasts of the field. To see starving orphans on TV—it wrecked her. She didn't understand that modern life . . . just to exist in it requires a certain hard-heartedness, right? You had to function within the awfulness surrounding you, divorcing your soul from the worst of it. Of course, if you kept your soul too distant—if it was just a buoy tethered to your corporeal being—well, you became a sociopath, just like our boy. Franny had never formed that stony wall around her heart.

My shoes made no sound as I walked down the corridor to the day room. The tiles at the facility were made from special rubber that muffled the *tak-tak* of hard-soled shoes, on account of some residents being peculiar about sharp noises. The TV in the day room was bolted to the wall, too high for anyone to fiddle with the channels; the CBC was broadcasting an old episode of *Seeing Things*.

Two guys in one corner were playing Chinese checkers. One of the players had an eye patch and kept putting the marbles in his mouth; his partner snorted, as if this was an everyday occurrence, and said, "Stick them up your asshole, why don't you, and lay a fucking egg." His opponent seemed to be legitimately considering this opportunity until a big-bull orderly said, "Don't even think about it, Gene. If I have to go digging again, I'm gonna stick a cork in you when I'm done."

Franny sat at a patio table draped in a big yellow parasol, even though we were indoors. Her face broke into pure sunshine when she saw me.

"Look at you," she said. "A million bucks."

"No, *you* look like a billion bucks."

"You look like a trillion, like—"

"Infinity."

We'd spoken the word at the same time. *Jinx.*

"So, Fran, I—"

"You broke the peace, Blake," she said solemnly. "You owe me a Coke."

I paid for two sodas from the vending machine. As I returned to the table, my eyes homed in on the scar above her temple.

The day it happened, we'd gone to Lakeside Park with our father. There was this woman with a spider monkey in a wire cage. It had on a dress with a frilly waist like a ballerina. The woman wasn't charging anything; she just wanted the attention. Sitting off to the side was her daughter, who had the dirty-kneed look of a kid who could do with a proper bath. Franny made faces for her, got the girl to break into giggles, but kids that age, they're like pigeons: feed them once, they won't leave you be. When we had to go the girl burst into tears. Her mom gave her a swat while the monkey screeched like hell.

On the drive home Franny started crying, too. My father tried to comfort her but she was inconsolable. She couldn't see why the monkey would get the biggest bite of that woman's love. That girl was her kid. It's a wonder she didn't dry up like an old leaf, for all the tears she shed.

Later that afternoon I heard a metallic rattle against the siding, followed minutes later by a heavy crumple. I ran out front to find Franny on the grass. My father's big ladder was tilted against the side of the house, all the way up to the roof.

"Baby birds were chirping up in the eave," she told me in the hospital weeks later, when she came out of her coma. "I had to check if their mama was being good to them."

Whatever dark melancholy Franny suffered from, that fall ended it. She broke one of the plates in her skull and the shard of bone obliterated two tablespoons of brain matter. But it must have been the most troubling matter, because Franny was instantly "cured"—if cured meant being left without a care in the world.

"Did you bring a book of matches?" she asked me now.

"No, Franny. You know I didn't."

"You said you would."

"You know I couldn't in good conscience. Not after all that happened, sis."

"What happened?" she said, pretending she really didn't know.

"You and matches don't agree."

She crossed her arms tight and said, "Oh, pooh."

Franny was sweating—another after-effect of the fall. She perspired constantly like a foreign cheese, the beads alighting on her brow and on the smooth skin under her eyes—most heavily when fire was involved.

By most yardsticks, Franny was truly better off. Her angst and existential dread had fled. But other changes were more troubling. For example: if you lit a fire in front of her, a queer glow would come into her eyes. Before the "accident"—the whole family referred to it as such—Franny had been afraid of fire. The first time she'd caught me on the porch burning the edges of the White Pages with a magnifying glass, her hands had fluttered like startled birds.

"You're going to burn yourself," she said. "You'll need skin graphs like Michael Jackson!"

Jackson had recently burned his hair off on the set of a Pepsi commercial. Franny—who was highly intelligent but very literal—had envisioned a team of eggheads hovering over the immolated pop superstar, plotting graphs on his skin.

But after the accident, her fascination with fire verged on obscene. She'd collect fallen twigs from the backyard maple and light fires on the grass. She'd steal coins from our father's pockets to buy wooden camp matches. I'd find her on the porch with a Zippo, her nostrils dilated to inhale the perfume of lighter fluid, sparking the wheel with her thumb—but not quite hard enough to light the wick.

A couple of years later, she'd started disappearing at night. Around that same time, the reports had began to surface.

"Can I ask you something, Franny?"

She traced her finger around the rim of the Coke can, dabbed her wet fingertip on her throat. "Of course, silly."

"Someone's been setting fires, Fran. A lot of them."

Back when we were teenagers, a rash of suspicious fires had coincided with Franny's midnight forays. At first they were nothing serious: dumpster blazes, or a stack of pallets incinerated on a warehouse loading dock. But anyone with an understanding of pyromania could spot an escalating boldness.

One July night, I had awoken to the smell of smoke. I went to Franny's room and found her lying awake on top of the covers. Her nightgown was stained with sweat. The pads of her feet were grey with ash.

"Don't tell," she said.

But I *had* told, despite it feeling like a betrayal. I couldn't shake the image of Franny dashing down dark streets at the witching hour, her nightgown flapping around her bare ankles, a bottle of butane in one hand and her Zippo in the other. A beautiful wraith setting the city ablaze.

"Who's setting fires, Blake?"

"Well, Franny, if I knew who, I'd stop him."

"Why?"

"What he's doing is dangerous. People have died."

Franny stared at her lap.

I said, "Have you been talking to anyone here about fires lately?"

She shook her head with a vicious side-to-side movement. Her gown slipped and uncovered the burn scar over her clavicle. The skin was the mottled pink of carnival taffy. She'd done this to herself in the facility's washroom, sprinkling hardware-store thermite on the toilet seat and lighting it. The reaction had fused the plastic to the porcelain, sending up a cone of superheated gases that had burned through muscle and fascia to scorch the wing-shaped bones next to her throat. The wall of her carotid artery had ruptured, but the afterburn had fused it shut; she'd only lost a few pints rather than the whole bottle.

After that, photos of Franny had been distributed to area hardware stores, convenience stores, and drug marts with a warning: *Do not sell flammable materials to this individual.*

"You'd tell me if you heard anything, right, Franny? If you knew someone was playing with fire?"

"I don't know that I would, Blake."

"Why not?"

"Did you know that carbon is the chemical building block of all known life on earth? There are only so many carbon atoms on our planet—no more today, right now, than when it all started."

I didn't like it when she got this way. Calm and logical.

"It's true. Things are born, they exist, expire, break down to their elements again. Carbon atoms don't die; they just get recycled. They go on to be part of new life. So, you see, all of us are cobbled together out of carbon cells that were once other things entirely. You could have a trilobite's tail in your elbow, or a cell from Attila the Hun's moustache in your eye. Any creature to have taken on life, grown, crawled, run, learned, known, felt, loved, or any of that. Carbon. Isn't that a wonderful idea?"

"It's not an idea. It's a fact."

Franny chewed her lip. "But you agree that it's wonderful?"

"Sure. I can agree."

"So you agree that when things burn, they get brought back to the beginning? The awfulness is gone. From there, something beautiful can spring up ... because too much of what we have is ugly. I don't mean ugly on the eyes, brother. Ugly on the *heart*. Evil and cruelty and things that gut the soul. But when you burn them, only the potential is left. Just carbon. And carbon isn't inherently anything."

"Oh, Fran. Don't the creatures living right now, you and me and our family and friends—don't we deserve to go on living until nature decides?"

Franny started to cry, which she did often and effortlessly. Her heart was an imperfect pearl, lacking the necessary nacre.

"I wish it could be like that," she said. "But nature doesn't have its head screwed on right. I wish the whole world would burn. You and me, too, even though I love you so much. I wish the earth was a black ball, all charred up. It could be that way for a few million years, and then new things would start to spring up. Things that would be better."

Franny's tears ceased abruptly, like a sprinkler shutting off.

"Oh, hello, Blake," she said, and her face broke into sunshine again. "When did you get here?"

Cataract City kept on burning. Houses, schools, walk-in clinics. The St. Ann church on Buchanan Avenue collapsed on itself; the church bell crashed through the narthex and melted into a pool of stannite.

My boss took a stress leave; there were rumblings that he'd be fired. I figured he would accept a quiet shit-canning: Almost overnight, his hair had gone white.

And still nobody saw anything; it was as if the fires had kindled out of pure nothingness.

The *Niagara Gazette* circulated a theory that we were under attack from militant anarchists—*What Are Your Demands?* one breathless headline read—until its printing press got torched. The overtly religious believed that Our Boy (he'd earned the capitalization by then) was the devil himself. Even the faithless were inclined to agree.

One night, a squat apartment block, the Portwood Arms, burned to the ground. Our Boy managed to string fifteen jugs around the Portwood's perimeter without being spotted. By the time the residents clued in, the fire had curled around the gas mains, which ruptured in gouts of blue flame and scattered the exterior brickwork over a three-block radius. Flames swept up the telephone poles to the transformers, which exploded in a gibbering of sparks, the wires catching like fuses as lines of polar whiteness—the distinct colour of an electrical fire—zipped from pole to pole across the city grid.

By the time the fire trucks arrived, residents were leaping from their balconies. Some had snapped ankles, some had spiderwebbed kneecaps. The firefighters did their best to catch jumpers with the trampoline, but some of these leapers were more ash than skin. The firefighters were beat to hell anyway; the station-house poles were getting more use than the poles at the strip clubs down Lundy's Lane—one of which had caught fire midway through a Saturday night disrobing: Bucktoothed men and willowy, half-naked women had spilled from the exits like solar flares released from a sun's glowing-hot corona.

I paid numerous visits to the burn ward. Gurneys were strung down the hallways, and the air hung with the acrid tang of burn ointment.

Clifford Meggs, said the name on one chart clipped to a bed. Thirty-eight years old. Resided in suite 344 of the Portwood Arms. I recognized him as the junior partner at a local law firm.

Meggs was a WASP, but parts of him were presently charred black. Charcoal-briquette black. When silica sand is heated to extreme temperatures, it becomes obsidian: black glass. Human skin performs pretty much the same trick.

"Got a smoke?" Meggs asked.

His hands were swaddled in bandages. I lit a cigarette,

inhaled to set the ember aglow, placed it between his lips. Meggs just let it burn.

I tapped the IV bag hanging on a pole above his bed. "Methadone?"

Meggs said, "No pussyfooting around, bro. I told them to give me the whole hog. Morphine. Self-administered."

"How?" I asked, nodding at his mummified hands.

"Button's between my toes."

Gingerly, I tented the sheet off his feet. Son of a gun. Meggs smiled—an incremental lift at the edges of his mouth, on account of the terrible burns on his neck.

"I'm a fire investigator, Mr. Meggs. I want to ask you about the other night."

For an instant, I thought my request had surprised him. Then I realized he'd be wearing that same semi-shocked expression until his eyebrows grew back.

"I didn't leave my stove on, if that's what you're wondering."

"No, no, we're positive it was an outside instigator. What I'm interested in, Mr. Meggs, is what you might have seen."

Meggs's eyes closed. His eyeballs quivered behind vein-wormed lids. Without opening them, he said, "Ash me, would you?"

I tapped the ash off his cigarette. His eyes didn't open as his lips accepted it back.

"Thanks. Now, you're asking did I see anything. The answer is yes . . . but you're going to think I'm crazy."

"You seen the state of our city lately?"

"Point taken. Well, Mister."

"Kennedy. Blake Kennedy."

"Well, Blake, I believe I saw a woman in a nightgown."

My heart gave a hard little kick—*ba-dum!*

"My kitchen window faces south over the Falls, right? I leave the window open at night to catch the sound of the water over the rooftops. I was at the window drinking a beer when I saw, or think so . . . a woman. In a nightdress. Some kind of gauzy material that you could *juuuust* about see through, but not quite . . ."

"Was she—?"

Meggs cracked one eye. "Carrying a torch? Yeah, although I can tell you weren't going to ask me that. A lit torch, just like an Olympian. It left a contrail same as a jet leaves high in the sky. I've never seen anything move so fast . . . a heartbeat after she passed from sight, flames were climbing up to kiss me good night."

"Could you describe her?"

"Any more than I just did?" Meggs rotated the cigarette from one side of his mouth to the other. "Not so it'd stand up in court. But if you plunked her down in front of me?" He gnawed agitatedly at the filter, and the blackness on his neck cracked open to reveal shocking veins of red. His drip must've been dialed sky-high. "But I don't think she's the one you're looking for."

"Come again?"

"You're looking for one person, right? A lone firebug."

"The assumption is—"

"What if it's a bunch of people, bro? A whole city?"

"I don't take your meaning."

Meggs swallowed. The working of his Adam's apple resembled the tunnelling of a beetle under crusted soil. "I'm going to tell you something, but if you hold me to it later I'll say it was the drugs I'm on, right?"

"Go on."

"The other night, I followed a stranger home. Yeah, I know. Weird. Didn't know the guy, just passed him on the street like I've passed ten thousand other guys . . . but something about this guy was different. Nothing you could put a finger on. I was just . . . curious. Wanted to see where he lived. What kind of car he drove. If he had a family. I followed him down Wiltshire to his house on Harvard. He went inside. I walked back towards my own home. But I kept thinking about the guy. He had a pigeon-toed gait. That intrigued me."

Meggs's face contorted. "I can't tell you what I was thinking. I can only tell you what I did, which was find myself at the PetroCan station off Dorchester, filling a jerry can."

He shivered, and now a line of flesh split open across his forehead. I wanted to tell him to calm down, but I needed to know.

"I had this . . . *fantasy* is the only word for it. If I set his house on fire, he'd jump into my arms. I'd save him. He'd be grateful, and we'd . . . the fantasy dissolved from there. I came to—like from a dream—at the gas station.

High-test was spilling over the lip of the jerry can and soaking my shirtsleeve."

My hand groped under the sheets and found the button between his toes. I pushed it. I pushed it again. Again.

"What are you doing?" he slurred.

"Nothing. It's okay."

"Jesus," Meggs rasped. "You can't ..."

His voice trailed to a thin whisper, then cut off entirely. I caught the cigarette as it slipped from his lips, then pinched off the ember between my thumb and forefinger. I fixated on the black spots on Meggs's face, watching him breathe. The skin underneath shone baby-pink. Fresh green shoots could push themselves up from that dark loam, right? A new version breathing itself into existence.

＝＝＝

Next, they burned down the barbershops. The air hung with the reek of fricasseed hair. Then they torched three fire trucks—half the city's fleet, burned in the firehouses while the firefighters slept upstairs. A parking lot full of police cruisers went off like chained firecrackers. Ambulances were next. A city bus rolled down the street with flames licking from its blown-out windows, shedding passengers from its doors, the driver nothing but a blackened effigy heat-welded to the shotgun seat.

They. By now I was convinced it had to be a team effort. That kind of wide-ranging destruction ...

The Armed Forces strung themselves down the Niagara River, bivouacking against the head of the Falls. What did soldiers know about fighting fires? Nothing, it turned out.

Someone lit up the whale tank at Land of Oceans. Floated a sheen of mineral oil on the show-pool's surface and set it ablaze. The whale, Neeka, couldn't surface to take a breath through her blowhole; the ambient gases would have roasted her lungs. She suffocated.

I called CMHA to speak to my sister.

"Were you out the other night?"

"No, Blake. They don't let me out unsupervised."

"That doesn't mean you weren't out, does it?"

"Don't talk to me like an infant, please."

"I'm sorry."

"What are you worried about?"

"Can't you see, Franny? The city's on fire."

"Of course I can see. I saw it all along."

"What the hell are you—?"

She hung up. She always did when I used curse words.

Soon my job became redundant. I had turned into an Armageddon investigator—and really, what value was that at the End of Times? It was like a weatherman sticking his hand out the window to tell you it's raining.

Strangely, nobody left town. Oh, there was the odd short-timer with kin outside the city limits who took a powder—but the locals all stayed. You'd see their haunted faces hovering behind windows, scanning the night for blooms of flame. I stayed, too. Even considered buying a fiddle.

The forests banding the river went next. Silhouettes of flame danced upon the surface dark of the water. Afterwards, the trees were nothing but charred pikes sticking out of the ground, the daggery teeth of some enormous subterranean monster.

The army gave up trying to guard anything and went in to clean up the mess. When the soldiers' utility shovels bit into the earth, fresh flames leaped up: the fire was still smouldering in the tree roots, waiting for the ground to open up and let it out again. Soldiers died, though the army never publicly reported how many.

The gunner on a patrolling Humvee shot an old man in an alley. Apparently, he'd snuck out to smoke his pipe; his wife refused to let him smoke indoors, figuring if her house was earmarked for ashes it ought not to be her hubby who did it. The gunner was twenty-one years old and by all accounts as flighty as a hummingbird. He opened up with the roof-mounted .50 cal, pumping a belt of copper jacket rounds into the alley. There wasn't much of the old man left to bury.

Finally, the army pulled up stakes. Ostensibly, they were re-strategizing, generating a fresh tactical matrix, but in reality they were abandoning us. They had been fighting ghosts, and losing badly. The city and all of us left inside it were collateral damage. In the end, it was just us. The good people of Cataract City.

Backdrafts form the backbone of every firefighter's nightmares.

Picture a room. One window, one door. Hardwood floor. One big, overstuffed chair—a La-Z-Boy, something like that.

Say that chair catches fire. It'll burn merrily, creating thick, hot smoke that spreads across the ceiling. Embers will ignite the hardwood veneer, bubbling and pocking the laminate, burning between the slats.

The gases will evolve—that's the scientific term— become saturated with heat, turn flammable.

A strange thing will happen: the flames will drop, like a gas range turned down low. All you'll see is the barest ripple, incandescent blue waves flickering over the floor. The fire has used up the oxygen, you see. It's starving. But at the same time, it's intensifying, each molecule tightening. It's finding just enough air to survive; and it'll pull in that breath from under the doorway and around the windowsill. The fire's a cockroach, doing anything to survive.

The fire becomes the equivalent of a man trapped underwater. If he stays under too long, he'll die—and so it is with fire. In a few days, you could open the door and all you'd get is a buffet of warm wind. But if you open it when the fire's desperate and let it take a big inhale . . .

A backdraft is what happens when a sleeping fire wakens. Its harbinger is a comical *whooooof*, like the bark of a St. Bernard. Those evolved gases ignite and expand, a quintillion superheated balloons bursting. Nobody can describe the experience of a backdraft; the first breath you take—a shock inhalation—will broil your lungs. Backdrafts don't leave witnesses.

The horror of a backdraft is that you never see it coming—but it's been there a long time. Waiting for you. Primed. It waits in the places you've known all your life. Those rooms of fondest acquaintance. The places you've felt most safe.

I walked the shattered city to find her, and as I walked the blackness of the earth leached into the sky, a dark imprint on the undersides of the clouds. I knelt beside a little pile of sticks that someone—perhaps a child—had assembled before abandoning it.

I ran a strike-anywhere match along the sidewalk and touched flame to tinder. Idly, I watched its small pyre burn.

Franny's facility was empty. The staff had deserted it. Rooms lay vacant, and in those rooms, beds had been torched down to the naked springs.

I found my sister on the roof. The city stretched down the alluvial slope to the Falls, which sparkled whitely in the twilight. Cataract City was the only place I'd ever known. I'd been born at its hospital, played Little League ball at the Lions Club diamond, kissed Laura Crowchild on the bleachers behind Westlane High. All ashes now.

"Hello, Blake."

"Hello, Fran."

"Did you know," she said, "that we're all the same, chemically speaking? Everything starts as hydrogen. Every living thing on earth. Carbon and nitrogen and oxygen—the chemical building blocks of life."

"You've told me this already, Franny. Many times."

"No, that was different. Listen. Please. These chemicals came out of a fusion process that takes place in the centre of suns, where the heat is twenty-seven million degrees. Humans are one of a trillion atomic by-products of that intense heat. Think about it, Blake: we all hail from stardust."

"That's a nice thought."

"It is, isn't it? But we fuck it up. It's our nature."

When we were kids, Franny used to pinch her skin hard enough to draw blood. When I asked why, Franny said she was waiting for it to shed the way a snake's did. She'd hoped that one night it would fall away and underneath would be a new face, not her own. I'd wondered, why would she ever wish to be something other than what she was?

She took my hand. The sleeve of her nightgown was frayed. Those threads would ignite without much effort at all.

"I've read about towns disappearing," she said. "It can happen overnight. No explanation. The fabric of a place dissolves. Entire families vanish. Some awfulness is visited upon the citizenry." Her fingers tightened around mine. "But what if the awfulness is something hidden inside themselves? Something they recognize, their collective awfulness?"

Flames nibbled at the periphery of my vision. The silky crackling of fire.

"Franny, we're not all bad."

"This part of us is."

"What part?"

Her arm made a vague sweep that took in the whole of the city. Then, with one finger, she pointed through my skin at my beating heart.

"It wasn't anything you could have beaten, Blake. All this was bound to happen, regardless."

Understanding, like a spark. Fire was always waiting, patient as a weed, to take us back to our base elements— back to stardust. Given a long enough timeline, everyone will pay what they owe. Cities are no different. Fairness doesn't factor into this story.

We stood on the roof, my sister and I. Waiting.

ACKNOWLEDGEMENTS

This collection has been a long time coming. Its first story to find a home was written in 2010, when I was living in Fredericton eking out a living as a newspaper editor. The last was finished this past year in Toronto, and informed by my perspective as a husband and father—and it arrives fifteen years after my first book, also a collection, hit the shelves.

A lot changes in fifteen years.

Certainly the things that interest me as a writer have. Nowadays, I have the strange sense—similar to how looking at an old yearbook photo (that hair! those bizarre fashion selections!) can prompt a rueful shake of the head—that early readers of my work will open these stories and think: How tragic. Davidson's gone soft as a marshmallow!

Maybe so. As I enter my mid-40s, I feel I have departed far from the starry-eyed 29-year-old who published his first collection. The road I've travelled has been a good one for the most part, and I've been grateful to travel it. But like all roads, all journeys, it marks you. So I hope those few odd souls who remember my first collection will see these new stories as the work of someone at a different place in his life. They are less the stories of a questioning and distempered twentysomething (with all the power of that age, too, and the boldness, the who-gives-a-shit-ness) than those of a husband and father with dreams and hopes and disillusionments and fears implicitly linked to this, my current stage in life. If I publish another collection twenty years from now (as far-off and hard to conceive as that may be) then I suppose I'll be writing the sort of stuff my own father might now find intriguing as story fodder.

One of the most poignant parts of a writing career, and likely all careers, is that it's not quite what you imagined it might be. Nothing in life is, though, is it? Before my first collection was published I figured that the people involved in bringing it to life—my agent, publisher, editor, publicist, the entire apparatus that took me in—would remain the same always, in much the way that my father worked at the same bank for his whole career. It is slightly distressing to discover that the names I mention below are (aside from my mother and father and now-wife) entirely different from those in the acknowledgements of a yellowed copy of *Rust and Bone*. But again, isn't that life? And while I hold some wry sorrow for my younger self and his naivete, I also believe that as a writer and a person you do, with luck, eventually find the people you work best with and trust most deeply, who foster your best work yet hold you to task when needed, and push you towards being better than you might otherwise be if left to your own impure devices.

So while most of the names that follow can also be found in the back pages of my last four books, I hope you will accept the repetition, knowing that this is tribute to my good fortune in finding them.

But first: Aside from "One Pure Thing," these stories were first published elsewhere, and so I thank those venues and their editors. The literary journal landscape is a fraught one, but the conscientious and thoughtful edits provided during the first publication of these stories was incredibly helpful and I am grateful.

As always, my thanks to my wife, Colleen, and our son, Nicholas, and our daughter, Charlotte. I can't do what I do without you, and to a great degree what I do *is* for you. Thanks, too, to my mother and father for their tireless (and I do mean tireless) support and love.

At Knopf Canada, thanks to Rick Meier, for all he does. And thanks to Deirdre, Melanie and Brett for their copyediting and proofing, and generally helping to round this manuscript into shape. Thanks to Andrew Roberts for his perfect cover.

Thanks to Kirby Kim, the bestest agent there ever was. And finally, thank-you to Lynn Henry, my editor, who always bats cleanup in these acknowledgements. I realize how lucky I am to have you. All the writers under your sheltering wing do. My gratitude is depthless.